Prais

"Awyn has written a bea
and personal empowerme
and rituals inviting the reader to hone their magical skills while
they explore their inner landscape. The book itself is laid out
as a kind of journey with each chapter going a little deeper to
discover healing and transformation.... People new to the craft
will find an easy entry point with Awyn's detailed instructions,
and experienced practitioners will find many novel ideas and
reminders to deepen their practice."
—**JOANN CALABRESE**, author of *Growing Mindful*

"This book is for those of us wishing to break out of our self-
imprisonment in all its various forms. Profound changes can
be brought about by cheap, simple rituals that are created and
experienced with sincerity and hope in our hearts that this
time they will work. Tricky subjects such as addictions, self-
sabotage, forgiveness, and enrichment are presented in a clear
and realistic style. You may not end up as a Mistress or Master
of the Universe, but *111 Magic* should go some way to making
your own world better."
—**GERALDINE BESKIN**, co-owner of The Atlantis Bookshop in London

111
Magic

About the Author

Awyn Dawn is a Pagan high priestess who has been working with spiritual seekers for nearly ten years. She has a BS in integrative health care from MSU Denver, an MFA in creative writing from City, University of London, and is Reiki II attuned. The author of *Paganism for Prisoners* and *Paganism on Parole*, Awyn is also a member of the Society of Authors and the Royal Society of Literature. Visit her at AwynDawn.com or follow her on social media @AwynDawn.

Awyn Dawn

111
Magic

Spells, Rituals, and Meditations
to Reclaim Your Power

Foreword by
Granddaughter Crow

Llewellyn Publications
Woodbury, Minnesota

First Edition
First Printing, 2024

Book design by Christine Ha
Cover design by Verlynda Pinckney
Interior illustrations by the Llewellyn Art Department

Photography is used for illustrative purposes only. The persons depicted may not endorse or represent the book's subject.

Llewellyn Publications is a registered trademark of Llewellyn Worldwide Ltd.

Library of Congress Cataloging-in-Publication Data
Names: Dawn, Awyn, author.
Title: 111 magic : spells, rituals, and meditations to reclaim your power / Awyn Dawn.
Other titles: One hundred eleven magic
Description: First edition. | Woodbury, Minnesota : Llewellyn Publications, [2024] | Includes bibliographical references. | Summary: "Shape the direction of your life and step confidently on your spiritual path with 111 spells, rituals, and meditations. This beginner-friendly guide teaches you how to create a safe space, work spells with the elements, meditate on spiritual archetypes, and empower yourself through the moon, sun, and planets. This book helps you grow spiritually and live more magically"—Provided by publisher.
Identifiers: LCCN 2024017138 (print) | LCCN 2024017139 (ebook) | ISBN 9780738773575 (paperback) | ISBN 9780738773728 (ebook)
Subjects: LCSH: Incantations. | Magic. | Spirituality.
Classification: LCC BF1558 .D39 2024 (print) | LCC BF1558 (ebook) | DDC 133.4/4—dc23/eng/20240509
LC record available at https://lccn.loc.gov/2024017138
LC ebook record available at https://lccn.loc.gov/2024017139

Llewellyn Publications
A Division of Llewellyn Worldwide Ltd.
2143 Wooddale Drive
Woodbury, MN 55125-2989
www.llewellyn.com

Printed in the United States of America

Other Books by Awyn Dawn

Paganism for Prisoners
Paganism on Parole

For all those who are changeable and shapeable, flow with the currents, and wax and wane with the moon.

For all those who are continuously working to become the best version of themselves.

And for those I've loved who have crossed the veil.

Contents

Workings

Foreword

In numerology, the number 111 has many meanings. To me, as a witch, magician, and shaman, it means "The beginning of the journey to connect with the divine creator within you." Regardless of how short or long you have been on your magical path, this book would make a perfect addition to your bookshelf. As a reference guide, a magical cookbook of spells, or a fundamental part of your magical practice, this will be a great part of your collection. I believe that life is like a lotus that unfolds with endless levels. So are we—a lotus that continues to unfold endlessly. There is always something new to dip your toe into. If you are at the end of one unfolding, you are at the beginning of the next. So am I.

Working with spells, rituals, and meditations will assist you with reclaiming your life, your experience, and yourself. Shakespeare wrote, "To thine own self be true."[1] I believe that Awyn understands this poetic stanza, as she provides tools to empower you on a personal

---

1. William Shakespeare, *Hamlet*, act 1, scene 3, Folger Shakespeare Library, https://www.folger.edu/explore/shakespeares-works/hamlet/read/1/3/.

level and hopes to positively affect humanity, one person at a time. This book is written for you and is a staple of your magical book nook. Philosophy has an expression about knowing yourself and therefore knowing the universe. Awyn provides us with spells, rituals, and meditations that will assist us with self-knowledge. She shows us how to use our voice, our mind, and our focus to tap into a magical, empowered path to reclaim our power.

She provides spells and rituals that help us to connect with our five basic senses, with the four elements, and with the cosmos. As within, so without, and so much more. There is so much information and perspective within this book. Awyn reminds us of healthy boundaries and spiritual ethics. She assists us in understanding that we all grow at different paces, that one pace is not right or wrong. The beauty of life is that we can develop individually and collectively. If you are a tree, you may grow slower than a flower. If you are a flower, you may grow faster than a tree. There is no right or wrong; the process of growth is individual, and Awyn provides tools for each of us.

Through Awyn's life experience and journey, she has taken notice of the idea that society would like us to fit nicely into a box, and most of us don't fit into this box. I do not fit into a box, and nor should you. Each of us is different, like snowflakes. This is the wonder of life in all the differing seasons that we are in. From a shamanistic point of view, the winter is not better than the summer—it is all a part of life. Awyn understands this and is here to assist us with all of life's paths, challenges, and ultimately our empowerment along the way. For it is all natural. She reveals to us that we all have the power to experience life, and that it is a hero's journey.

The mindful workings that she brings guide us to ourselves—not good or bad, not right or wrong. Just be yourself. "I am that I am."[2]

---

2. Exodus 3:14 (King James Version)

It is okay not to be okay. It is okay to grow, and there is a truth about "growing pains." Picture yourself in a gym, working out your muscles. Sometimes pain means gain. From a shamanistic point of view, I would ask the tree, "Tree, are you comfortable with the winds in your life?" The tree speaks to me, "It is the wind that makes me stand stronger." I would ask, "Tree, what happens with the harsh weather that comes?" The tree speaks to me, "It is not personal; it teaches me, if I am willing to learn and grow."

Awyn Dawn helps us to embody magic for both practical and soul workings. This book provides a menu of spells, rituals, and meditations that will benefit your life. She provides us with the basic, elemental, and reality-based perspectives of life to show us that life has magic—you have and are magic. She is very down to earth and connects with us in a very grounded way that simply makes sense. She is a breath of fresh air. She assists us with understanding how the universe connects with us on a personal level. Yes, you are a child of the universe, and it sends you signs, symbols, and numbers to connect with you. Like a road map, this book meets you at every twist and turn within your journey to empower you to be the best version of yourself that you can be.

If you are at a crossroads within your life, look into each of these chapters. There you will find empathy, understanding, and encouragement to grow from where you are. I cannot express enough that you are understood by Awyn. Life is not supposed to be easy. Life is here to assist you with being the most empowered that you can be. Your story is worth its weight in gold—this book is a support to assist you to be your empowered self.

Life is difficult. Awyn understands this and has approached this book with spells, rituals, and meditations that can assist with the hard times. Hard times are just that—a part of life. It is how you move through these hard times that can make a difference. This book can assist the reader with moving through hard times to become empowered and to create magic. In reviewing this book and the 111 spells, rituals, and meditations that are provided within, I am not only inspired by a wonderful person who would take the time to share this wisdom with us; I am encouraged by the individuals that I dream will be drawn to pick this book up. We are connected.

From my heart to yours, Awyn is here to inspire you, encourage you, and empower you to be your authentic self. This book is your guide to be your greatness, as only you can be.

Granddaughter Crow

Introduction

Magic may seem like something new, but like energy, magic always has and always will exist. Many, myself included, see energy and magic as one and the same. In the last couple of decades, there has been an increasing interest in Paganism, magic, the occult, numerology, tasseography, tarot, runes, spirituality, the afterlife, and so on. This revival, combined with the accessibility of information in the technological age, has fed many a curious mind and allowed seekers to set foot on their quest for spiritual growth.

Seeing numbers in a pattern, such as 111, is one of the ways that we can know the universe is communicating with us. Numbers make up the basis of everything. Now, I am no mathematician; in fact, math is very much a four-letter word to me. But I do know that the universe, in its vastness, is not going to speak with me in English. It will instead use signs, symbols, and numbers to speak. The number 111, though synchronistic on its own, is also a combination of the number 1, for beginnings, and the number 11, which signifies a spiritual awakening and finding inner strength. When we combine these concepts, it indicates the full circle of a journey. As you read this, you are at both a beginning and ending phase in your life. This book is designed to help you navigate the parts between where you are and where you hope to be.

Throughout this book, you will find spells, meditations, and rituals—111 of them—that are going to encourage you to examine your spirituality and the different aspects of yourself in a deep and meaningful way. This is not work to be undertaken as an afterthought. The number 111 reminds us that personal growth lies in the hands (and spirit) of the individual. We are not helplessly and haplessly floating around, awaiting life to do what it wants with us. We have the ability to shape the direction of our lives, put ourselves steadfastly on a path, and give it our all.

Inspiration for This Book

When I first found magic, it came from Wicca. Like so many, my faith was surface level for a long time. I wore black and covered myself in pentagram jewelry because I thought this was what spirituality meant. Then, I was given the opportunity to step through the doorway of change. In my case, it came as an ultimatum. As a result, I now find myself with the kind of spiritual connection that won't waver but is still flexible and open to new ideas. I find myself not having to cling to the idea that Paganism, in any of its forms, comes from external items like clothes, tattoos, and jewelry (though they can accentuate it). You might say that I wear my symbols in the very cells of my body. Through this work, I have been able to begin the lifelong process that allows me to see my good attributes, my not-so-good attributes, and everything that lies in between.

As a society, we are becoming increasingly uncomfortable with being uncomfortable. There is an expectation, it seems, to have everything we encounter fit into our comfort bubble. We never want to be a little too hot or a little too cold. We never want to experience sadness, pain, or heartache. While I certainly want everyone to lead a life that is full of happiness, I also want people to grow. I want you to become the most radiant and magnificent version of yourself that you can be. You won't get there if you skirt around everything that takes you out of your comfort zone. You must go through the darkness, through the discomfort, through the processes that challenge you mentally, physically, and spiritually to truly emerge into the light. As you read, give yourself permission to laugh and smile and have fun, even with the most serious bits. Yes, the work is deep, but you don't have to be miserable. It works better if you're excited by the prospect of growth.

If this sounds like too much, it's okay. You can dip your toe in bit by bit. The spells and meditations within these pages do not need to be followed in an A–Z order. You can do one exercise, some of them, or all of them, and you can go through them in any order, though they do progress in depth as the chapters go on. The gods and goddesses will guide you to find what you need. When going through meditations and rituals, do the best you can. Some people have a harder time with visualization and an easier time with chanting, for example. If you come up with an idea for how to adapt the spells to better fit your skill set, then please, adapt away. It is more important to do the work than to worry about it being done "correctly."

On Working with Others

You will probably notice that most of the spells provided are set up for the solitary practitioner. This is because the focus of this book is on working on oneself. If you want to work with a partner or in a group setting, these practices can be adapted to fit multiple people. Be advised, though, that people are going to experience spiritual growth at different rates. Resist the urge to insist that another take part in these exercises if they are not willing. If your partner, friend, or family member doesn't want to participate, that is okay. They may or may not change their mind later. The same applies to you. You can stop at any time for any reason, or no reason at all, and pick up the practices again when it is time.

It can also be tempting when working with someone you care about to put their spirituality ahead of your own. This usually comes with good intentions, but you know what is said about roads paved with good intentions. For this reason, I encourage you to undergo this work with your healing and your growth in mind. If you want someone else to change, all you can do is lead by example and hope for the best.

How to Use This Book

This book is to help people get the benefit of working on themselves by providing meditations, spells, and rituals that focus specifically on self-growth and healing. Magic has the potential to empower humanity one person at a time. Meditation connects us to the gods and our inner world. Spells connect us to our world and give us the ability to change what we can. Rituals and ceremonies remind us to give thanks and have gratitude for this incredible set of experiences called life.

There are 111 exercises you can do in this book. You do not need to do all 111 to benefit from this book. You can go through the exercises one by one, or you can move around throughout the book. You can repeat exercises if you enjoy them, and hopefully you will. The exercises you don't do will be waiting in these pages should you change your mind and want to come back to them later.

The exercises get progressively more challenging, especially around chapters 6 and 7. This doesn't mean you can't skip ahead, but the chapters are in order for a reason. You should at least familiarize yourself with the work in chapters 1 and 2 before moving on, as these exercises will help you establish your foundation.

The meditations in this book vary in complexity. I suggest that before you complete a meditation you read through it. Then, either record the meditation and play it back, or have a friend read it to you while you are in your meditative state. This will save you from having to open your eyes to see what comes next, thereby breaking your focus.

Shopkeeping

Before you embark on this new adventure, there needs to be a bit of shopkeeping.

Land

Whenever you are working in the natural world, attend to it with respect. While no one owns land in the cosmic sense, they do in the legal sense. So if you bury anything, go anywhere wild for your rites, or make offerings to the earth, do so only in areas where you are allowed to be. The rules of the trail apply: if you pack it in, take it out. This means leave no trash and don't vanadalize, destroy, or ruin that space. Be respectful.

Candles

First and foremost, a lot of spells in this book call for leaving candles burning. I know that everyone knows not to leave candles burning unattended, but I will mention it anyway: Do not leave candles burning unattended. Animals get curious or wind blows in through a window, and they tip over. Accidents happen. To avoid accidents, use fire safety sense. You can snuff your candle and relight it later, or at any time, you can substitute an electric candle. If available, use candles made of natural wax, especially if you will be burying them. I don't specifically list candleholders in most of the exercises, but they should be a given. After all, you can't leave a candle floating in air.

Essential Oils

Essential oils seem harmless, and mostly they are if they are used properly. That being said, if you get a pure essential oil, it should be mixed with a carrier oil, such as almond, grapeseed, coconut, or olive. Pure essential oils are quite potent (and can be expensive). They can irritate the skin and bypass the blood-brain barrier. Many oils are premixed with a carrier oil, and some will tell you on the bottle. If you go to a shop where they blend oils, someone who works there can tell you if it is blended or not.

When in doubt, get out a piece of paper. Dab a bit of oil on the paper. If the oil evaporates and doesn't leave a mark on the paper, then it is a pure essential oil. You can mix it with roughly 1 drop of essential oil to 1 teaspoon carrier oil.[3]

Throughout this book, you will also see references to oils for deities or concepts, such as Freyja and compassion. Local apothecaries and metaphysical shops often carry blends, can create blends, or can recommend a worthy substitute. If these shops are not accessible to you, you can look online for herbs, flowers, and scents with similar

---

3. "Here's the Best Way to Dilute Your Essential Oils," Abbey Essentials, August 4, 2020, https://abbeyessentials.co.uk/blogs/news/heres-the-best-way-to-dilute -your-essential-oils.

properties and substitute them. Also remember, extra-virgin olive oil can always be used instead.

Common Sense

Lastly, I want to talk about common sense and magic. It would not be possible for me to provide a disclaimer for every single scenario that could happen in life or ritual. It is up to you to be accountable and to use common sense. It should not need to be said that you should not ingest anything not edible or that you should not do these exercises while driving. If you are reading this book, it means that you want to grow and become empowered. Part of that means thinking things through. I encourage you to apply that to each spell, ritual, meditation, and chant in this book.

Final Notes

This book can be used by those with little to no magical experience, those who are adept, and everyone in between. That being said, there may be some terms that you are not yet familiar with. I have included a glossary in the back of this book to provide brief, general definitions. If you come across a term you want to know more about, I encourage you to read and research and ask questions. You will notice that a lot of the work in this book is up to you to do. This is how life works; you get out of it what you put into it—not in the sense of working yourself into an early grave, but in the way of experience. Sure, you can always choose to shelter from the rain, but what will you learn by dancing in it?

Dance well, dear readers. Dance well.

Chapter 1
Creating a Safe Space

The spells, rituals, and meditations you will perform in this book can get intense, to say the least. It is important for your growth that you create a safe space for transformation to happen. Different types of safety will be discussed in this chapter. Some you have probably considered before; others may be new to you. The exercises go beyond physical safety and include making a sacred space for your sacred practice to happen.

In a perfect world, we would all have a room that was dedicated for magical purposes and could stay as sacred space all the time. In the world where most of us live, we will have to get creative. Maybe you reserve a specific time of day when your family agrees not to use the bedroom. If you have young children, consider either including them in some of the simpler rituals or planning your work around their bedtime. The point is, you do not need a twelve-room house to make a safe or sacred space. You can use a corner, a closet, a bathroom, or whatever you have available.

What Makes a Space Safe?

There are many ways to look at what makes something safe. Safety is more than just a locked door. When you ask yourself, Is this a safe space? I want you to consider the mental, emotional, spiritual, physical, and magical aspects of safety. We are going to look at these briefly just so you have an idea of the context of this book. Refer back to these as a reference whenever you need them.

Mental: Mental safety refers to your state of mind when you head into ritual or meditation. I want you to know that *everybody* has days when they do not feel mentally up to par. It is okay to not be okay. I cannot decide for you what being in a good mental space looks like, but I will say that if you feel like you shouldn't perform a certain spell or meditation, then don't—at least not right now. You can always change your mind about it later.

Emotional: Much of what applies to mental safety also applies to emotional safety. If you find a ritual and you feel like it will bring up memories and emotions you are not ready to face, skip it for now. If you just lost a pet or experienced a breakup or job loss, then today probably isn't the best day to work on healing trauma. Luckily, I have included a Bad Day Spell in a later chapter for you to utilize in such circumstances.

Spiritual: Are you supported on your spiritual path? If not, do you at least have a space where you can honor your spirituality without fear of judgment? Not everyone you meet will understand your longing to explore what is often called "alternative spirituality." You may not even understand it fully yourself. But as long as you can meditate, perform rituals, cast spells, or even just be in sacred space without fear of repercussions, that is a great start.

Physical: This is probably the easiest type of safety to understand. Can you be in your space without incurring physical harm? This may seem silly to ask, but while working through this book, you may find yourself working with candles or in a bathtub. Common sense and awareness of the elements can be the difference between having a delightful meditation and being pulled out of your meditation by the sound of something catching fire. (I've had that happen, by the way, and I would recommend preventing it whenever possible.)

Magical: There are a lot of fun elements to magic. One of the big attractors of people to Paganism is that we celebrate our faith instead of mourning it. Visit any number of the thousands of magical social media pages that exist and you will find easy, whimsical spells designed to delight. Magical safety should still be on your radar though. I'm not saying this next part to scare you or dissuade you, but not every spell and energetic being is in your best interest. Magical safety includes asking yourself if you have the necessary skills to perform that spell you found. Have you taken the time to ground and center beforehand? Have you meditated on potential outcomes? Are you ready for the potential consequences, be they positive or not, of this spell? Ask yourself, Are you willing to grow? Are you wanting to change?

The Importance of Breath

Breathing deeply and with intention is one of the simplest ways to combat stress. Most humans, especially in the Western world, live in a state of stress. Now, stress has a time and a place. Think back to early humans living in a world where we could become prey for many types of large animals. Stress, caused by being in the presence of a large animal, enables our sympathetic nervous system to activate. In layman's terms, the energy that would have gone toward digestion gets diverted to help us run from the animal and live another day. Once the threat has passed, the autonomic system resumes its functions. The problem is that our minds and bodies react to "getting yelled at by my boss" stress and "running from a tiger" stress in the same way.

When we are constantly under stress, functions such as digestion, reproduction, and emotional regulation take a back seat. As you breathe deeply, you will also cue your brain to release endorphins (feel-good hormones), stimulate your brain's electrical activity, and provide a window for your organs to return to homeostasis. By focusing on your breath for just a few minutes every day, you can release the stress that humans in the modern world are prone to carry and gain many health benefits.

It is for these reasons that I recommend you start every ritual, meditation, and spell with several deep, intentional breaths. A lot of people use the counting method. You simply breathe in while counting to five in your head. Then you hold for a count of three. Breathe out for five, and hold for a count of three. Repeat this until you feel relaxed. If you find yourself being weighed down by an extra-stressful day, add a visual element where you breathe out the stressful situation. If you do nothing else, utilizing this exercise for ten minutes will help restore many basic health functions.

1: Meditation to Breathe Away Stress

This meditation is what I like to call a *moving meditation*. That means you do not sit but are encouraged to move, stretch, and expand and contract your body. Stress lives in places like our muscles, so moving our muscles essentially helps squeeze out the stress. You know your body and the movements it is capable of, so adapt this meditation to fit within your movement abilities. If you have a physical condition that might prevent you from being able to do the exercise safely, skip it. Your safety is a priority. If you are good at visualizing, then incorporate visualization into this meditation, seeing yourself breathe out your stress. If you share your home with anyone, you may choose to tell them you need ten to fifteen minutes by yourself to complete this meditation.

Begin Meditation

First, stand with your feet shoulder-width apart. Bounce a few times and shake your shoulders to loosen up. Once you have wiggled around for a minute or two, it is time to incorporate breath.

Take a deep breath in, filling the bottom of your lungs, and roll onto the balls of your feet. You should feel a slight stretch in the back of your legs. Hold for a few seconds. Now breathe out slowly, and slowly come down onto your whole foot. Breathe in, and on your next breath out, roll onto your heels. Once again, you should feel a slight stretch. Breathe in, and roll back onto the flats of your feet. Repeat this four more times, for a total of five times.

Return to your original position, feet flat and shoulder-width apart. As you breathe in, gently shift your weight to your right leg and breathe out. On your next breath in, shift to your left leg and breathe out. Repeat this five times on each side.

As we move up the body, I want to remind you that none of this should hurt. The intent is to provide a slight stretch and not traumatize your body.

Next will be the back. This is a particularly sensitive area, so slight movements are key. As you breathe in, bend back slightly, and as you breathe out, return to standing. On your next breath out, lean forward. Then as you breathe in, return to center. Repeat this for a count of five.

For your shoulders, you will want to roll them backward in circles while focusing on your breath—in and out. Breathe in and out five times, then stop. Start rolling your shoulders forward and repeat the process of breathing. You will use this same method for your neck. Start counterclockwise, breathe in and out five times, then stop. Repeat the motion, this time clockwise for a breath count of five.

Next come the arms. Start by holding them bent at chest height. As you exhale, stretch them out so your hands are each open, palms toward an opposing wall. When you inhale, bring your hands toward your chest. As in the previous exercises, you will do this five times before you release the stress in your hands.

Your wrists and hands can be shaken out in a way that feels comfortable. Then while you exhale, stretch your hands wide. While you inhale, bring the tips of your fingers together. Then for five breaths, rotate your wrists toward each other and away from each other for another five.

When you get to your head, you will want to use your hands to release the stress carried in your facial muscles. You can do this by kneading your hands around your face and head while you take a series of deep and conscious breaths. Be sure to focus on high-stress areas such as your temples, cranioverterbral junction (where the neck meets the head), temporomandibular joints (jaw), and around your eyes.

When you are done, check to see if any areas of your body still feel tight or tense. If so, repeat the stress reduction movements for that area. Once you feel all the stress has been released from your body, return to the original position with your feet square under your hips. Close your eyes. Take a deep breath in, then breathe out fast with a whoosh. Breathe in and breathe out a little softer. Then on your third breath, return to normal breathing.

This stress reduction technique can be done in many different settings. A lot of humans find themselves living a largely sedentary lifestyle. This moving meditation has the added benefit of encouraging blood flow and the oxygenation of various organs. Try to do this several times per week.

2: Ground and Center

If you only get good at one thing magically when you are starting off, it should be grounding and centering. Think of an electrical outlet. It has energy flowing through it, but there is also a grounding plug to keep the outlet from overloading. When you ground and center, you are like that outlet—connected to the universal energy but grounding out the excess so you don't get overwhelmed. After you practice for a while, you may get to a point where you can just think about your need to ground and center and it will happen.

Until you can do this easily on your own, you can use this exercise or any other variation you like. Any spell or meditation done in this book can be started with grounding and centering and circlecasting (included later in this chapter). I am including an example here so that you may come back and use it as a resource.

What You Will Need
+ The only thing you need is you

Preparation

This works best if you are either barefoot or can touch the ground. However, if you are on the subway, at work, or just someplace you can't take off your shoes, you can still perform a grounding and centering. If possible, though, try to touch something directly connected to the ground, such as a wall or the metal bar on the subway.

Instructions

Sit on the ground with your weight on your sitz bones (the bottom of your pelvis). Make sure they are firmly connected to whatever you are sitting on. Sit with your back tall and feet flat in front of you or folded onto one another in half-lotus position. Focus your attention on your breath. Make sure you are breathing deeply and into the bottom of your lungs as you did in the last exercise. Try not to force your breathing; just let it come.

After you have taken several deep breaths in and out, draw your attention to the base of your spine. On your next breath in, imagine a green light from your lungs traveling into your spine. Then from your spine, you "see" it connecting you to the earth through your sitz bones. This may take you several breaths. That is fine; this is not a race. All things in their own time.

When you feel that you have established your connection to the earth, keep breathing, and with each inhale, see the light making its way deeper into the earth. One breath may take you below the crust, another through the mantle. Keep going until you reach the core of the earth. Then keep breathing, but this time you will be moving the light out the other side of the earth. Breathe until you break through the crust on the other side.

Now, this light that started at your tailbone and has made its way through the earth will start to circle back toward you, moving around the outside of the earth, picking up energy along the way. It circles around until it reaches the crown of your head. When it reaches your skull, begin to breathe that energy into your body. Notice if you get any sensations, such as the light changing color, changes in your body temperature, and other similar experiences. Breathe in and out until the light fills up your whole body and connects back to the base of your spine.

Now, to center, you will imagine this light making its way to the center of your body, usually a spot just below your ribcage and just in front of your spine. Gather the energy here, at your core. This is your reserve of energy. You may notice that not all of it gathers here; some may stay in other parts of your body, particularly your extremities. Let it be. Energy flows where it needs to.

Bring your attention back to your sitz bones. Start to become aware of where you are and the world around you. Let the sounds and smells return you to the mundane world. But know that you are no longer drained by it or giving it your energy. You are being fed by the limitless supply of energy that resides within the cosmos. When you feel you are back in the mundane world, open your eyes and slowly allow yourself to move around.

How to Pick a Physical Safe Space

While it is not always possible to be safe everywhere you go, you can create a safe space in your life to experience transformation. The most important factor is that you will be relatively undisturbed. Infants will cry, people will knock on the door, and the day you are trying to work on personal growth will inevitably be the day that a construction crew has to dig up the sidewalk right outside your house. But to whatever extent possible, the space should give you enough privacy to focus on what you are doing.

Go through the types of safety. Mentally tick off each one that your space meets. Remember that emotional safety depends on you and your state of mind. Once you have a space that meets the criteria, one that you feel safe getting vulnerable in, you can get to work cleansing it, creating it, and casting your protective circle.

Altar Creation

An altar is not a requirement for most of the exercises in this book. I can't even tell you how many times, for whatever reason, I have laid a cloth on the floor and designated it my ritual space with great success. Whole books could be written on altar creation, but for the purposes of this book, I am going to keep it simple. An altar is your magical working space. That's it, in a nutshell.

Traditionally, your altar will have an altar cloth to cover it, then a representation of the four elements (see glossary) and spirit. On mine, I also have two seven-day glass candles. The black one on the left represents the sacred feminine and the white one on the right represents the sacred masculine. Then I keep a chalice and plate. I also have a small cauldron that I use as a fireproof container. I keep a lighter in the drawer so I never have to go searching.

Last but not least, I place my athame horizontally along the south edge of my altar. Some people use a wand instead; it is up to you. While there are differences between the energy of a wand and an athame, and reasons for choosing one over another, that discussion goes beyond the scope of this book. So let's leave that for another day.

This is not an exhaustive list, but it is a good guideline if you have never set up an altar before. Not all practitioners choose to have one. If you choose not to, you can easily substitute a flat table (I still recommend covering it with a cloth) and use that to set up your materials.

Cleansing Your Safe Space

Once you have found your safe space, you will need to cleanse it. I have provided several different ways to do this. Each uses a different technique: the four elements, smoke, or sound. Choose what works for you.

3: Cleansing Your Safe Space with the Four Elements

In this first version of the cleansing ritual, you will use the four elements—earth, air, fire, and water—to create a space that is cleansed by the power of these elements.

What You Will Need
+ A few pinches of salt in a bowl
+ Water in a cup
+ Patchouli or sandalwood incense
+ Lighter or matches

Preparation
Start by grounding and centering yourself as described earlier in this chapter.

Instructions
Take three pinches of salt and add it to the cup of water. As you do, say, "Earth and water, elements of the sacred feminine, lay the foundation on which I will build this space, lending it strength and intuition."

Then, working your way from the north point of the room and going in a widdershins (counterclockwise) motion, repeat the words as you sprinkle the salt and water mixture throughout the room.

Return to your starting point. Now light the incense stick. Let the smoke waft where you are for a moment. Then say, "Fire and air, elements of the sacred masculine, build upon this foundation, lending it thought and creativity."

Then, working your way from the north point of the room and going in a deosil (clockwise) motion, repeat the words as you let the incense smoke waft into each corner of the room.

Return to your starting point. Point to the floor below you, and using your pointer finger, draw a pentagram there. Say, "By the elements below, this space is cleansed."

Point to the ceiling above you, and using your pointer finger, draw a pentagram there. Say, "By the elements above, this space is cleansed. May it ever remain so."

4: Cleansing Your Safe Space with Smoke

The practice of using herbs to clear the air within a space has existed cross-culturally for thousands of years. The practice of smoke cleansing, sometimes called *smudging*, existed in different variations across Europe, parts of Asia, and, of course, in certain Native American cultures.[4] But the specific rites used by each of these cultures—the gods, goddesses, spirits, and entities called upon, and the herbs used—varied from place to place.

Many herbs have cleansing properties, so do not think yourself limited to sage. If you do opt to use sage, be aware that the white sage variety, *Salvia apiana*, has largely been overharvested. Only buy ethically sourced white sage or, better yet, use an alternative. Rosemary (*Salvia rosmarinus*), sage (*Salvia officinalis*), clary sage (*Salvia sclarea*), juniper (*Juniperus communis*), blue sage (*Salvia azurea*), and yerba

---

4. Alethea Cho, "The Ancient Art of Smoke Cleansing & an Interview with a Scottish Smudge Maker," Medium, SweetWitch, November 28, 2019, https://medium.com/sweetwitch/the-ancient-art-of-smoke-cleansing-an-interview-with-a-scottish-smudge-maker-6d97f37af899.

santa (*Eriodictyon californicum*) can all be used instead in either bundle or powder form.

What You Will Need
+ An herb bundle (or powdered herbs)
+ Lighter or matches
+ Fireproof dish
+ A bowl with a bit of honey and a cinnamon stick in it
+ *Optional:* charcoal disc if using powdered herbs

Preparation
If you are using powdered herbs, you will want to light the charcoal disc in the fireproof container and let it get going for about five minutes before you add the herbs.

Instructions
Start in the center of your room or as close as you can get to it. Take a moment to ground and center yourself. Light your herb bundle, then walk in a widdershins spiral while chanting,

> *Hestia, goddess of home, goddess of hearth,*
> *By fire cleanse my piece of earth.*
> *Keep this place in sacred peace.*
> *Keep this space sacred to me.*

In your mind's eye, see the smoke chasing out any unwanted energetic residue above, below, and all around you. (Please note that herb bundles tend to go out. If this happens, just relight it and continue.)

When you get to the edges of your room, you may not be able to walk in an exact spiral, so follow the spiral shape as best you can along the walls of the room. When you get to doors or windows, pause for a moment, draw a pentagram with the smoke, and say, "By Hestia, this space is secure."

When you have circled the entire room, return to center. Place your herb bundle in the fireproof container. It should go out on its own. If it doesn't, you can tap it out after the ritual.

Standing there in the center of your room, pick up the offering bowl with honey and cinnamon. Say a prayer to Hestia, something to give her thanks for protecting your home, and dedicate the offering to her. You can say whatever words you feel like saying, or simply say,

> *Hestia, goddess and guardian of my home,*
> *I offer to thee this gift of honey and cinnamon*
> *In hopes that your protection will be ever constant.*

Leave the offering bowl by the front door or on your hearth. If you are unable to leave it there on a long-term basis, leave it overnight, then bury it as close to your front door as you are able.

5: Cleansing Your Safe Space with Sound

This is an extremely versatile ritual that can be adapted to be used for any space, vehicle, item, etc. In this case, though, you will be cleansing your working space. This adaptation is especially useful at times when leaving a candle or incense burning would not be viable. While I recommend a singing bowl, you can use a drum, violin, flute, or any instrument that has a good vibration when you play it. You also don't have to be a professional musician. You just need to be able to play a note.

What You Will Need
   + A singing bowl and wand (or other instrument
     mentioned above)
   + *Optional:* a singing bowl pillow

Preparation
If you have never used a singing bowl before, there are two ways you
can do it. Both will require you to have the bowl either on a pillow or
in the palm of your hand with your fingers stretched away from the
bowl so you are not cupping it. The simplest way is to tap the side.
The other, preferred, way is to apply pressure to the wand while you
run it around the lip of the bowl. Practice these techniques a few times
before you begin. If you are using an instrument with which you are
unfamiliar that is not a singing bowl, spend some time learning how
to use it.

Instructions
For this ritual, you will start at the door of your space and use the
vibration from the bowl to scatter any unwanted energy. Move
widdershins around the room, stopping every few feet to let the energy
of sound fill the space. If you are finding it difficult to play the bowl,
you can tap the side with the wand and wait until the vibration stops
before moving on.

   Work your way around the room until you are back at your
starting point. You should be able to feel a change in the energy of the
room. It will almost hum with the new vibration.

6: Do I Feel Safe Meditation

The following meditation is designed to help you attune with your chosen physical safe space and get a sense of the energies within it. This will give you an idea if the space needs another cleansing (never a bad idea) or if it is ready for you to go ahead and do your work.

You should be barefoot for this meditation. Make sure that you will be undisturbed for the duration of it. Stand in this area that you will be devoting to your spiritual work. Have your feet bare and flat on the ground and your arms outstretched. Then begin.

Begin Meditation

Breathe deeply into your lungs and close your eyes. First, check in with your body. Are there any parts of your body that feel sore, achy, itchy, or uncomfortable? If so, acknowledge this. Then decide if you want to go forward with the meditation. If you do, checking in with the physical space will be your next step. You are looking for the energetic footprint or vibration of the space. You may receive information in a variety of ways, such as sound, smell, messages ... Try not to compare your expectations with reality. Just let the information come to you.

Starting at the doorway, put your hands out in front of you. What do you feel? Is the space in front of the door warm? Cold? Comforting? Maybe you don't *feel* anything per se, but are you overcome by an emotion? Do you see a color or shape in your mind's eye? Pay attention to all the sensations you get, even if they seem small or you feel like they should be insignificant. When you are first learning to incorporate magical and spiritual practices, the information you receive may be little more than a whisper. So you'll have to pay attention.

Once you have received the energetic imprint of the doorway, move clockwise slowly around your space with your hands open, palms in front of you. Just as you did with the doorway, close your eyes and ask yourself what impressions you are getting from a certain area. Perhaps your wall connects to the apartment next door. This wall may have a different energy about it than the rest of the room. Make a mental note. Circle all the way around the room until you are back at your starting point.

You're not quite done though. We are three-dimensional beings that exist in a three-dimensional space. Walk to the center of your room and put your hands, palms up, toward the ceiling. Again, you are looking for those energetic footprints and feelings. Lastly, you will turn your attention to the floor. First, feel the energy. Then, place your palms flat on the floor. Send any extra energy you picked up down into the earth. This works even if you are in an apartment with several floors below you. However, if you do not feel grounded after this, put your hands into a potted plant instead.

7: Spell to Create a Safe Space

After cleansing your space, you may find areas of your space feel mucky or like they have "weird energy." To remedy that, you are going to clear out any iffy energy and claim it as safe space. If you are using an area that also serves another purpose (i.e., bedroom, office, or living space), you will want to re-cleanse and reclaim it periodically.

There are multiple parts to this ritual. There is the grounding and centering, as discussed earlier, then a specific cleansing ritual, followed by a circlecasting and dedication of your space as sacred.

What You Will Need

- ✦ Representation of the god or goddess you want to protect your space. Statues work best, but 2D images can also work if that is what you have.
- ✦ Incense

- A dark blue taper candle and candleholder
- Lighter or matches
- Some salt in a bowl
- Water
- An essential oil for that deity
- Cakes and ale

Preparation

Before you begin the ritual, you will want to have a safe place to keep your deity statue or representation. You should set them up facing the main doorway so they may see all who enter. Make sure this is a spot where your deity will not be disturbed or knocked over. If you have felines, this may involve having a conversation with your cat beforehand.

Light your incense and candle. Ground and center yourself.

Instructions

After you have completed setting up, you will want to energetically cleanse your statue. Take three pinches of salt and add it to the water. Splash a few drops on the statue and say, "By earth and water, thou art cleansed."

Then run the statue through the incense smoke and above the candle flame, careful not to burn it. Say, "By fire and air, thou art cleansed."

Next, you will hold up the statue in front of you with both hands.

I call on you, [deity name].
I ask you to be here as I dedicate this space to you.

Anoint the statue with oil. (A little goes a long way. A few drops are fine.) Place the deity in their place of power.

From here you shall see all things, sense all things,
  and know all things.
I dedicate this space to you, [deity name].

Leave the cakes and ale until your candle burns down or until the next sunrise. Then dispose of the cakes and ale by offering them to the earth. Dispose of candle remains in an eco-friendly way.

8: Circlecasting and Dedication

Not every Pagan tradition casts a circle. You might want to consider casting a circle if you want extra support when performing a ritual or spell or if you will be going into a trance or deep meditation. It not only provides safety; it makes your space a sacred one. This can be used with the safe space ritual or on its own. You are going to be doing work on yourself that will not always be comfortable. Casting a circle can help you feel protected. You might also want to cast circle if you are in a strange or unsafe area, even if you are doing simple meditations. Even if you feel safe, you might want to cast a circle to signify the beginning and end of your rite. I am including one version of a circlecasting, both opening and closing, that you can use with any spellcasting, meditation, or ritual.

What You Will Need
   + 1 green seven-day glass candle
   + 1 yellow seven-day glass candle
   + 1 red seven-day glass candle
   + 1 blue seven-day glass candle
   + Lighter or matches
   + Candle snuffer or lid
   + *Optional:* If you do not know what direction north is, you will want a compass or app that can tell you.

Preparation

Locate north (using a compass or app if necessary). Then set up your candles to correspond to their direction: the green candle will go in the north, then yellow in the east, red in the south, and blue in the west.

Instructions

You will start in the north and go to each candle, following the actions and saying the words for each direction. When you speak, do so with authority, not fear, though you may feel it the first time. Remember, you are not quietly asking for the guardians and elementals to please show up when they have time. You are commanding them to stand in a position and stand guard to keep you safe. You don't have to be rude, but you are giving an order.

Start in the north to lay your foundation. Squat down and put your hands on the earth, but look straight ahead and say,

> *Guardians and elementals of the north, stand steadfast*
> *as the earth within this space.*
> *Be my protectors and watchful eyes so that none may*
> *enter that I do not abide.*

Light the candle and say, "Welcome."

Move to the candle in the east. Breathe in deeply, smelling the air, letting it fill you, and say,

> *Guardians and elementals of the east, blow swift as*
> *the wind within this space.*
> *Be my protectors and watchful eyes so that none may*
> *enter that I do not abide.*

Light the candle and say, "Welcome."

Move to the south and light your match, watch the flame dance, and say,

> Guardians and elementals of the south, shine bright
>   as the fire within this space.
> Be my protectors and watchful eyes so that none may
>   enter that I do not abide.

Light the candle and say, "Welcome."

Finally, move to the west. Feel the water in your cells allowing them to move and expand and heal. Say,

> Guardians and elementals of the west, flow swift as
>   the water within this space.
> Be my protectors and watchful eyes so that none may
>   enter that I do not abide.

Light the candle and say, "Welcome."

Return to the north and stand in front of the northern flame. Hold out the pointer and middle fingers of your dominant hand so they are touching each other. Say the words,

> I am sovereign over this space.
> The circle I cast is unbreakable,
> Made from the elements of earth and air and fire and
>   water and spirit.
> I am protected in each moment, in all times that I reside
>   within.

Walk around the space chanting the words and visualizing a bright, white light coming from your fingertips to encircle you. Keep repeating the words as you walk the circle in the same direction you lit the candles until you are back at north. If you feel you need to repeat the chant, you may do so while walking the circle again for a total of three or five times.

Once the circle is cast, you may continue with your ritual knowing that you are completely protected. You can leave the circle up until you are done with your rite. Then it is customary to take it down. Some people leave the circle up all the time. But I like to open the space back up, as it can indicate the end of the rite.

The Take Down

To take down your circle, sometimes called *opening circle*, you will do what you just did, but in reverse. So instead of walking clockwise, you will start at the north and walk widdershins. Instead of lighting a candle, you will extinguish the candle, and so on.

You will start in the north, just as you did when casting. Using the same two fingers, you are going to walk around the circle and imagine the light dissipating into smaller, floating balls of light that eventually waft down into the earth or up into the sky where their energy can be reused. As you walk, say,

> *Protective circle, protective space,*
> *Return to the elements with my thanks.*

However many times you initially walked to cast the circle, walk that many to open it.

Then you will go to each candle, starting in the north and working widdershins, and say, "For your protection, I give thanks. Hail to you, that you may be on your way."

Then put the candle out with the snuffer. Do not blow the candle out. Air is the complement to fire, the element that gives it life. Instead, extinguish the flame with earth (the snuffer) or by putting a lid over the glass. You can reuse these candles next time you need the protection of the elements. Do this at each candle and return to north. Say, "This circle is open, yet it is never broken. Huzzah."

Chapter 2
Protection

In the previous chapter, you learned how to create safe space by cleansing out old and unwanted energies. Essentially, you gave yourself a clean palette to work with. I want you to remember that all of these protective spells need to be backed up with physical action. None of these spells can replace locking your doors at night and wearing a helmet when you ride your bike. What they can do is reinforce the safety measures you have already put in place.

As you work your way through this next chapter, avoid thinking about how the spells will work or why. Instead, know that they will work, then remove them from your mind. It is a mistake to live in a constant state of fear. That's not going to help you stay safe. Instead, be wise, be cautious, use common sense, and trust in the protective power of your magic.

9: Shielding

Personal shielding is an important skill to learn, particularly if you are a gifted empath and the emotions of others affect yours. Even if you are not, all day long you are exchanging bits of energy with people. When you have a shield (made of energy, of course), it protects your personal energy. If someone drains you every time you are around them, create a shield and they will pull energy from it instead of you.

What You Will Need
 + No items needed

Preparation
When you first begin learning to shield, you will want to be in a place where you can focus without interruption. As you become more practiced, you will be able to shield with more distractions.

Instructions
To begin, sit or stand in a comfortable position. Think of your favorite element: earth, air, fire, or water. Bring your attention to your feet. See that element swirling around you, moving its way up your body. It surrounds you, moving from feet to knees to hips to chest and head. It flows over your head and below your feet. It will surround you 360 degrees.

As it completely encircles you, it will slow and take on its natural state. So, for earth, you may see yourself surrounded by dirt or tree bark. If you chose water, you may find it to be like a flexible globe. If you are new to shielding, you will want to check in with your shield a few times throughout the day. Eventually, you will discover that it stays quite well on its own.

10: Spell to Keep Intruders Out

Home invasion is a reasonable fear for many people. This spell not only keeps out strangers who might rob you but can also keep out people who you know but who do not have good intentions. This doesn't mean a person who is mad at you temporarily, but those who generally do not have your best interest at heart.

What You Will Need
+ 3 ramekins or bowls
+ Extra-virgin olive oil, just enough to coat the bottom of one of the bowls
+ A few pinches of salt in another of the bowls

Preparation
Have the oil and salt each in their own bowls and the empty bowl sitting between them.

Instructions
Pour a bit of oil into the bowl and add a pinch of salt. Mix them together in a deosil direction with the index finger of your power hand (the one you write with). While you stir, see the bowl filling up with a bright, gold light.

At each door, window, or other opening to your home, dip your finger into the oily blend and draw a pentagram on the door itself or on the window frame. Your front and back door in particular should have the pentagram drawn in good size.

Each time you draw one on, use your voice of power (chapter 4) to say,

> *This space is mine,*
> *Protected now and for all time.*
> *None may enter without my permission.*
> *None may enter who cause suspicion.*
> *By the gods, I mark this home*
> *And designate it a safety zone.*

When you are done, offer any remaining oil to the earth and any remaining salt to the water.

11: Witch Bottle

Witch bottles date back to at least the sixteenth and seventeenth centuries, when they were used as a tool to trap negative energies and entities.[5] Only use one if you have a yard or outdoor space that is designated for your use. This bottle should ideally never be found. So if you share a yard with a neighbor who likes to garden, you might want to rethink that location.

---

5. Jennifer Viegas, "17th Century Urine-Filled 'Witch Bottle' Found," NBC News, NBC Universal, June 4, 2009, https://www.nbcnews.com/id/wbna31107319.

What You Will Need
- Red candle
- A double boiler designated only for magical purposes, or you can make one with a firesafe container in a pot of water
- Oven mitts
- Jar or bottle with a lid (A pickle jar is a good size.)
- Nails, pins, barbs, and other sharp objects
- Hair from each family member
- Nail clippings from each family member
- Urine or blood from each family member (It must be extracted without causing harm to the individual. Menstrual blood is a great option, but urine is easier to acquire.)
- Metal spoon
- Bowl to catch wax

Preparation
You may want to collect the fluid from your family members in one or individual containers beforehand. If they are all joining in the creation process of the witch bottle, they can opt to pee in the bottle after the other objects are added. However, it may be easier to collect the fluid in a different container and add it later.

Scout the area where you will want to bury your jar. Near the front door or at the beginning of your walkway are good options. If you live in an apartment, you can put your bottle beneath a potted plant as long as it doesn't have the type of roots that could break your bottle.

Instructions

Start melting your candle wax in the double boiler. Melt it slowly to avoid it burning.

When the wax is melted, place the nails and sharp objects carefully into the jar. Then add the hair and fingernail clippings. Then cover them with the urine from your family members. The objects should be coated with liquid, but it is okay if the jar is not completely full.

Put the lid on tightly.

Carefully coat the lid with melted wax to seal it. You can either spoon the wax on bit by bit, dip the whole top of the jar into the wax, or pour the wax over the bottle. Whatever method you choose, be careful, as the wax will be hot.

Once the wax cools, bury the bottle upside down in the selected location and cover it with dirt. Keep it there until you move, then dispose of it and make a new one for your new home.

12: Boundary Spell

Boundaries keep us safe; they are protective. This spell may remind you to protect yourself from toxic people and situations by setting and holding your boundaries. It was created by my good friend JoyBelle Phelan, a fellow Pagan and a longtime tarot reader.

What You Will Need
+ One of the following stones: clear quartz, black tourmaline, obsidian, hematite, or black jade

Preparation

To begin, hold your crystal in your hand.

Instructions

Imagine a boundary, whatever seems natural for you. It can be a shield or a castle wall or even a hedge of bindweed. See it surrounding you, encompassing you.

Speak aloud: "Negativity is cast out of my space. I am protected and at peace."

Imagine the boundary sending energy into your crystal. It is being imbued with the energy you are speaking, the boundary you are setting.

Dismiss your boundary and carry your stone as a reminder that you have set a boundary that honors your needs.

13: Wards

When you create a ward, you are imbuing an inanimate object with the energy of a protective being. Think about it as a representation. If you want a dragon to be a ward for your home, you will want to have a representation of that dragon. Even though it is not alive in the same way you or I are, it is alive in an energetic sense and must regularly be "fed" (with candles), wiped down, and kept in good condition. When you create a ward, it agrees to secure your home in exchange for being well-tended.

You will want to give some thought to the kind of being you want to protect your home. Read up on the lore surrounding it. Also, consider if you have the time to dedicate to caring for it. It is fun to want to fill your house with many wards, but will you have the time to clean them each week? Light candles for them? If they are wood, can you treat the wood regularly? Start with one ward. It will be plenty powerful for most homes.

What You Will Need

- ✦ A physical representation of your ward (I recommend using a statue. Dragons, gargoyles, tigers, angels, skulls, ravens, and wolves work well for this, but it can be anything you feel is protective.)
- ✦ Blood orange essential oil
- ✦ A conjuring incense or ground bay leaves
- ✦ Three chime or taper candles arranged in a triangle: one gold, one silver, and the third a color that represents your ward, such as yellow for a lion or red for a dragon.
- ✦ Lighter or matches
- ✦ *Optional:* You will also need a bowl of dirt or salt if you are performing the ritual inside.

Preparation

You will want to have a space dedicated to your ward before you start. Spend some time with them for a few days before performing the ritual. You don't need to take them everywhere, but do build a rapport. Maybe your ward likes music, chin scratches, or to spend time in the sun? I will say it again: Your wards, though statues, are alive in an ethereal sense. They have personalities and feelings. They will be with you for a long time. It will serve you well to get to know them. During the ritual, you will even find out their name.

Instructions

Start on the Sunday on or before a full moon. Take your ward into the sunlight; you can either go outside or stand in an open window or doorway. Using your dominant hand (your power hand), reach toward the sun. Feel its rays finding your hand. Now pull these rays down with your power hand as if you are pulling a rope. Use your senses to make these solar rays as real and tangible as you can. Bring your hands together until the energy takes on the shape of your ward. This shape will probably match the statue you have selected. Place your nondominant hand on the ward and visualize its energetic body entering the statue.

Add your power hand to your ward and see the energy finish entering it. Say,

> *As the sun gives life through warmth and brightness*
> *So too life is given to you.*
> *The sun's essence, its warming rays,*
> *Give you the spark of being for all days.*

Anoint your ward with blood orange essential oil.

Next, light your conjuring incense. Waft your ward gently through the smoke. The smoke will take on the rough form of your ward. As you continue to waft your ward through the smoke, see its essence entering the physical representation you have selected. Then say,

> *Air. Breath. Being.*
> *Breathe and be.*
> *Air. Breath. Being.*
> *Real you are to all and me.*

Set your ward on your altar or in another safe space until the full moon.

When the full moon arises, take your ward into the moonlight. This time, you will use your nondominant hand and hold your ward in your dominant hand. Just like you did with the sun, you are going to reach toward the moon and grab her essence. Again, use your senses to make these lunar rays as real and tangible as you can. Bring your hands together until the energy takes on the shape of your ward.

Place your nondominant hand on the ward and see the energetic representation enter the physical. Say,

> Silvery watcher of the night sky,
> Imbue this ward with reflective light.
> As you watch the shadows that dance in darkened night,
> So too will they watch with seeing eyes.

Take a pinch of earth or salt and place it on your ward's head.

> By earth that is my body,
> By earth that is yours.
> Real, tangible, manifest.
> Give me now your name.

Look at your ward, face-to-face. The first name you are given is their name. Hold them up to the moonlight: "I now name you [say the name that they told you]."

Set your ward between the three candles.

Light the gold candle: "Gold to give you life."

Light the silver candle: "Silver to give you influence on the physical plane."

Light the last candle: "The third to finalize it all and let the universe know thy name."

When the candles have all burned out, set your ward in their home location. Remember to feed them regularly by lighting an anointed candle near them and letting it burn down.

14: Safety Spell for Pets

We all want our pets to be safe. Knowing they are can help make our minds a safe place to grow, heal, and become empowered. Depending on if you are out of the broom closet with your faith and what flavor of Paganism you practice, you can use a symbol to help protect your beloved animal.

What You Will Need

+ Pet-friendly paint and paintbrush, or you can use a needle and thread (Brown works well, especially if you're using a simple symbol.)
+ Collar (If your pet can't wear a collar, paint the outside of their food or water bowl.)
+ *Optional:* water cup for brushes, pen or pencil, scissors

Preparation

Do some research beforehand to determine an appropriate deity to ask to protect your pet. For example, if you have a cat, ask Freyja, Bast, Ra, or Artemis to provide protection. If you have a dog, reach out to Anubis, Epona, or Lugh. If you have a small pet, such as a mouse or hamster, try Apollo. And for you snake people, there's Renenutet, Meretseger, Enki, Hathor, or the Minoan Snake Goddess, whose name has been lost to time. Choose a symbol that represents your deity or protection in general. I have included some suggestions, but you are not limited to these.

Pentagram

Equal-armed cross

Brighid's cross

Eye of Horus

Please note that if you will be sewing the symbol, especially by hand, start the embroidering beforehand. Just leave a bit of it unfinished so you can complete it in ritual.

This spell is best done on a Monday, Saturday, or Sunday.

Instructions

Lay the collar or bowl in front of you. Take a few deep breaths. If you want to trace out the image before you paint or sew it, do so now. If you are painting, try to use smooth strokes. Paint or sew a protective symbol onto the collar or bowl. If using paint, be sure to paint the outside of the bowl, not the inside.

As you do, call on the god or goddess whom you want to protect your pet. For this example, I am going to ask the Egyptian Bast to protect my cat, but the first line can be changed with the name of your chosen deity and your type of pet. You can visualize a protective blue light surrounding your pet while you call out,

> *[Bast, Bast, Keeper of Cats.] Be ever mindful and protective over [pet's name].*
> *Keep them safe from harm: human, plant, animal, and more.*
> *May they return ever to me, to their home, for all days that they will be.*

Repeat this chant over and over until you have painted or embroidered their bowl or collar and you feel that the charm is set. Repeat this as needed when the symbol wears away, if they need a new collar, or if they are given a new dish.

15: Safety Spell for Kids

For this spell, refer to the protective symbols shown in the previous spell. Choose one (or more) for your child. This spell, like the one before it, calls for sewing skills. If you do not have sewing skills, fret not. You can look for iron-on patches with the protective symbol. Or you can buy blank ones and use a Sharpie or fabric paint to add the symbol. The benefits of DIY patches are that you are putting extra energy into them and that you can also invite the wee ones to help with the task according to their age. If using paint or markers, you will want to put a towel over the patch when you iron it on to avoid burning or melting the symbol.

What You Will Need

+ A blue taper candle
+ Candle carver
+ A few pinches of ground frankincense
+ A small bowl of extra-virgin olive oil
+ Candleholder
+ Lighter or matches
+ An article of clothing, backpack, belt, etc. that the child will frequently have with them and hopefully won't lose
+ Needle and thread (or fabric paint or markers); blue or purple are preferred thread colors
+ *Optional:* a patch with the protective symbol

Preparation

If you are creating patches, get them started beforehand. If using paint, allow it to dry. If you are sewing a symbol without a patch, you can start it now. But if it is simple enough, consider completing it all during the spell. Consider if you want the symbol to be visible on the outside of the clothing or hidden inside it.

Instructions

Carve the name of the child (or children) you want to protect on the candle. Drop a few pinches of your frankincense powder into the oil and mix with the index finger of your dominant hand. Using two fingers, anoint the candle with the oil and powder blend. Think of the word *protect* or an image that means protection while you do so.

Place the candle in a candleholder and light the wick. Let the candle burn for a moment, then wash your hands.

When you return, pick up the article of clothing and finish stitching, painting, or drawing the protective image onto the item. With each stitch or stroke, say, "[Child's name], thou art protected from all harms magical and mundane."

When you are finished creating the symbol, leave the article of clothing in front of the candle, but far enough away to avoid wax drippings, until the candle burns out completely. Then give the item to your child. You can do this on multiple bits of clothing. It even works on socks, hats, and other such items.

16: Safety Spell for the Whole Family

As the name states, this spell can be used for full family protection. It is simple and effective. As in the last spell, you do not have to be skilled at sewing to make this work. Basic skills are perfectly fine, though many videos are available that can help you increase your skills.

What You Will Need
  + Black cloth, at least 2" x 2"
  + Needle and thread
  + 1 acorn
  + 3 of the following herbs: basil, angelica, black pepper, bay leaf, fennel seed, cinnamon, marshmallow root, mullein, or pine needles
  + A strand of hair from each family member (Alternatively, fingernails or a photo can be used.)
  + Gold paint
  + Paintbrush
  + A cup of water for the paintbrush

Preparation
Start by shaping the black cloth into a bag. Sew together three sides, leaving one end open. Turn the bag right side out after you sew it so that the stitching is on the inside.

Instructions
Fill the inside of the bag with the acorn, the herbs, and the hair. As you add the hair, chant that family member's name seven times and end by saying, "Thou art protected."

Once you have everything inside the bag, sew up the remaining end. Use your gold paint to draw the equal-armed cross (or other protective symbol) onto your bag. If you want to add a string or thread to wear it, do so. Keep the sachet you just made in one of your safe spaces. Repaint it as needed.

Chapter 3
Self-Exploration

One of the most challenging parts about encouraging a path of personal growth in your life is coming face-to-face with the stout realization of who you are. We tend to like to look at ourselves through a filter. Sometimes that filter highlights all our best attributes, downplaying our less-desirable qualities. Sometimes the inverse is true, and we struggle to see the positive attributes that we have. You might be saying to yourself, I already know who I am, and to a certain extent, that may be true. But this book is to help you go beyond what you think you know and help you attain a deeper understanding of yourself and the world that surrounds you. This is part of pathworking.

When the Norse god Odin hung himself from Yggdrasil and sacrificed himself to himself, what he was essentially doing was abandoning the idea of who he was to see himself in a clearer light. That is what you will learn to do in this chapter (without having to hang on a tree for nine days). We are all full of strengths and weaknesses that make us so deliciously human. It is when you see yourself as honestly as possible that you can step into your power and own who you are. This will be mentioned again in the chapter on empowerment, but you must know who you are before you can empower who you are.

17: Ritual to Call on Psyche

Psyche is the Greek goddess of the soul. She was a human and later made into a goddess, but her time spent as a mortal gave her unique insight into the essence of humanity. Since she is married to Eros, the Greek god of love, she can help you to identify and appreciate—if not adore—all the parts of you. This ritual is to get to know her, and in turn, get to know yourself. There is a meditation included as part of this ritual. You can use the meditation as a standalone meditation or within this ritual.

What You Will Need
+ A purple taper or chime candle
+ A candle-carving tool or boline
+ An essential oil: either sweet almond or lily
+ Candleholder
+ Lighter or matches
+ Paper
+ Colored pencils
+ Firesafe dish
+ An offering of honey and mead or white grape juice
+ *Optional:* moonstone or amethyst to keep on your altar or carry with you

Preparation
Carve a scythe on the candle with your candle-carving tool. Do not worry about it being perfect. The intent is to create a symbolic doorway into your mind.

Once you have carved the symbol, anoint the candle with oil and put it in the candleholder.

Instructions

Before you light the candle, sit facing it for a moment. Breathe in and out with intention as you ask Psyche to join you in this ritual. When you feel she has heard you, light the candle and say, "Welcome and blessings to you, Psyche."

Now pull out the paper and pencils. Take your time and create a butterfly on the paper before you. Do not rush. This is an image of transformation that you are creating, so invest some time and energy into its creation. As a final touch, write the words *body*, *mind*, and *spirit* in a circle around the image.

Hold this image close to your heart, then out in front of you. Using the flame from the candle to light it, burn this image in the firesafe dish. Watch as the smoke dances and swirls, taking your intent of transformation up to the gods themselves. Once the ritual is done, provide your offering of mead or juice and honey.

As an addition, you can include the Meditation with Psyche, given next. It was designed to complement the ritual. Then you can follow up with the Psyche Spell to create an assemblage of transformation.

18: Meditation with Psyche

This meditation is to help you understand transformation and how it applies to your life. When we undergo transformation, it can be empowering, scary, easy, or complicated. But it is, nevertheless, natural. Using the imagery of a caterpillar, you will learn that when you let yourself break down, you can be rebuilt into anyone.

Begin Meditation

Focus on your breathing for nine breaths. As you approach the ninth breath, visualize yourself sitting on a leaf on a tree. You are small but not insignificant. Feel the breeze coming in from the east. It dances over your skin. You look back at your feet and soon realize that you are not a human anymore, but a caterpillar, fuzzy and green. The world around you takes on a new importance and new meaning.

An instinct within you tells you to climb, so you make your way up the branch and climb up the bark of the tree. You find a small hollow that will shield you from any wind, rain, or predator. In the safety of this hollow, you make a cocoon for yourself. You wrap yourself in layer after layer of silk, which is both soft and strong. Here inside, you will have a place for your symbolic transformation to occur.

Once the cocoon surrounds your entire body, begin to dissolve all the parts of yourself. Feel your body soften and see the various aspects of yourself come forward. Some will be great... strength, forethought, and kindness. Others will be aspects that you may not want to keep, such as jealousy, anger, fear, and codependency. As all these parts swirl around in your cocoon, avoid the urge to critique or self-loathe. Know that we are all born with strengths and weaknesses. Also know that fear, in moderation, is lifesaving and has purpose.

As you begin to rebuild yourself, you are not striving for perfection, no. Instead, you want to highlight your strengths and become aware of your weaknesses. Put the pieces back together. You may notice that something you consider a weakness tags along and gets added to the form you are building. Brush off as much as you are able. But do not fret if some of your negative aspects come back. This cocoon is about preparing yourself for transformation, not completing it.

Once you are rebuilt, break free from your cocoon. You may at first see a small sliver of light. Put forward your hands, and expand that hole. Keep prying it open until you can step out, free, into the fresh air.

Standing before you, you see Psyche. She looks at you and sees your transformation; her face echoes her pride. She holds up a reflective drop of water. As you gaze into it, see yourself there, standing tall. Out of your back are two large wings. The colors that dominate them indicate the area of your life your transformation will first affect. Take note of these colors to look up later.

Psyche, still looking at you, speaks the word "trust." She is telling you to trust your wings. Flap them and feel yourself lifted into the air. Flap them again and go still higher. Though there is no ground below you, you know that you are safe because your wings, your transformation, will carry you.

After some time in the air, come back to the leaf where you began your journey. Feel your feet gently touch down on its smooth surface. Wrap your wings around you and close your eyes. It is time to come back to the physical world.

Begin to notice the floor beneath you and the weight of your body upon it. Then notice the temperature of the room and any scents or sounds within it. Notice the weight of your clothes on your body. When you feel that you are completely back in the mundane world, open your eyes and stretch.

Once you are out of meditation, sit in the space with Psyche. Do not rush to end the ritual. Stay and internalize all that has happened. When you are ready to leave, do so with thanks. Leave the offering in your sacred space as the candle burns down and out on its own.

It is important that you now eat nutritious food and drink water. Your body will need the fuel to feed the upcoming transformations.

19: Psyche Spell

This is a spell that allows you to ask for guidance from Psyche, especially during periods of transformation, and gain psychic growth. Remember that transformation doesn't always, or usually, come in like a crashing wave but tends to trickle in bit by bit. This can be used as a stand-alone, after the ritual, or before the meditation.

What You Will Need
- A purple taper candle
- Candle carver or boline
- Lavender oil
- Candleholder
- Some honey cakes or sweet bread
- Some juice, wine, or mead
- Lighter or matches
- A purple piece of jewelry or an item you can carry with you

Preparation
Carve the candle with the image of a butterfly. Then anoint the candle with lavender oil and set it in the holder. Set the honey cakes and juice in offering bowls off to the side.

Instructions

Take several deep breaths, light the candle, and say,

> *Goddess Psyche, I ask you to be here now,*
> *To guide me on my journey.*
> *Stay with me.*
> *Let me see the steps I need*
> *To take, to attain*
> *Psychic and spiritual growth.*

Dab a few drops of lavender oil on the jewelry and say, "This [jewelry item] marks my intent, my willingness, to follow the path before me."

Run the jewelry safely above the flame three times. Each time, visualize the purple light from Psyche's candle entering the jewelry item. Let it fill with purple light.

Lay your piece of jewelry at the base of the candle. Note that if it is too close, you might get wax on the item. If you want to avoid this, move the jewelry to another place on the altar before you leave the space.

Let the candle burn down, either somewhere you can watch it or in a safe place like a porcelain bathtub. Then put on your piece of jewelry. Whenever you wear this item in the future, you will be reminded that Psyche is with you, guiding you. So be sure to keep your eyes open for her signs that are sometimes subtle.

Put the offering outside or in the compost so it may return to the earth. Say thank you to Psyche as you do.

20: Discomfort Leads to Growth Meditation

In order to grow, we must get a bit uncomfortable. Consider the seed, buried beneath the earth. It opens in the darkness and goes upward. It fights through the soil, trusting that it will find sunlight when it finally emerges. If this seed had stayed buried in the comfort of the earth, it would never reach its full potential. See where I'm going with this? This meditation is designed to help you be okay with the discomfort that creates change. For this meditation, you will need warm blankets and comfortable clothing.

Begin Meditation

Cover yourself completely with your blankets, even your head. Close your eyes and feel the warmth that is wrapped around you. This is the warmth that tells a seed it is time to wake up. Stay wrapped and covered in your blankets; stay comfortable.

In a few moments, you start to notice that it is not as comfortable as it once was. How is the air? Is it stuffy? Is the warmth too warm? Stay wrapped until you get quite uncomfortable. Then, with your eyes still closed, sense the way you need to go to get back into the fresh air. Do not panic. Just breathe and slowly remove the blankets, first exposing your head.

Keep your eyes closed and take a deep breath. How is the air? Fresher than before? Crisper? Now remove yourself from the blankets. How is the room? Does it feel different? Open your eyes slowly and look around. This space: how has your perception of it changed? Even if just for a moment it was brighter, more welcoming, or more vibrant, then you have experienced the change that comes from allowing yourself to be a little uncomfortable. You don't have to always be uncomfortable; you are allowed to seek comfort. But do not automatically avoid all things that take you out of your comfort zone.

21: Personal Growth Meditation

Now that you have seen that being outside of your comfort zone can be beneficial, let's take a look at personal growth. This is a topic that is sometimes uncomfortable. Go into this meditation and the spell that follows it with an open mind, open heart, and a lot of self-love. For this meditation, you will want to relax and start off lying down if you are able to do so.

Begin Meditation

Curl yourself into a ball or the fetal position. If this isn't something you can do, put your hands or arms around your knees. Be as small as you can. Now, with your eyes closed, see yourself as a baby: Small, helpless, but everything is a fresh new experience. On the one hand, your bones are not even formed yet; on the other, life and all it has to offer is ahead of you. You are the potential that exists in the world.

What could you do as a baby? What could you not do? What thoughts and actions were yours, and what was yet to be developed?

Now fast-forward to early childhood, about six years old. Stretch your body just a little. You are starting to assert your independence but are still largely dependent on the adults in your life for your care. While you are not yet who you will be, you are beginning to form opinions, discover what you like and dislike, and have experiences that will shape how you view the world.

What could you do as a child? What could you not do? What thoughts and actions were yours, and what was yet to be developed?

This time, leap forward into those preteen and teenage years. Stretch out your feet and your hands. This is a time when we often feel conflicted and split. We experience life and culture beyond the boundaries of the home. The desire to be independent grows, yet you are not there. This is a time of great discovery and change in perception. The brain of a teenager begins to prune away what is no longer needed to make space for the habits and behaviors that will stay into adulthood.

What could you do as a teenager? What could you not do? What thoughts and actions were yours, and what was yet to be developed?

Now you will enter the years of early adulthood. Stretch your body out to its full size. This is a time when the freedom sought after by the teenager is finally realized and the full breadth of consequences are discovered. Still youthful and full of potential, the young adult is like the Fool of the tarot, setting out on an adventure but without the acquired wisdom of age. Though most young adults feel full-grown, time still has lessons to teach.

What could you do as a young adult? What could you not do? What thoughts and actions were yours, and what was yet to be developed?

Come to now, whatever age you are. This is the time for reflection. Consider each life stage and how you grew and changed with each transition. Did you learn from the folly of your younger years? What lessons do you still need to work on? We all have them. Learning is a continuous process that calls us down the path of the wise elder. The lessons repeat until we learn from them. So ask, What is repeatedly showing up in your life?

What can you do at your present age? What can you not do? What thoughts and actions are yours, and what has yet to develop?

Finally, fast forward to old age, whatever that means to you. Though this is a time when many of us lose flexibility and dexterity, we gain something much more viable: wisdom, the gift of age. The elders who have learned and continue to learn their lessons find themselves in a place to guide and impart sacred wisdom. You have no choice in aging, but you do have a choice in acknowledging the path of personal growth so that when you do age, you are ready to step into the elder role.

What do you want to be able to do at that age? What do you not want to do? What thoughts and actions do you want to own?

As you lie there in your future, sacred elder-self, see the limitations you had as a child, teenager, young adult, and in your present form falling away. Who do you want to be? What does that sacred, limitless form look like? How do you handle conflict? Death? Celebrations? Growth? Guidance? What needs to fall away from your current form to get you there?

Return to your current age. One by one, see these limitations (in the form of light or other physical representation) falling away. One by one, they detach and dissipate around you. When they are cast away, fill in the spot(s) they left behind with a silver, growing light.

Slowly start to bring yourself back into the physical world. Notice the room around you, the weight of your body on the floor. Become aware of any smells or other sensations. When you feel like you are completely back, open your eyes and sit in stillness for a few moments. It is okay and preferable to not start moving around right away.

As you go about the days and weeks and months that will follow, keep that elder version of yourself in mind. Consciously consider if each action you take gets you closer or further from that person.

22: Personal Growth Spell

One of the most well-known symbols of change is the frog. From an egg to a legless tadpole to its adult amphibious form, a frog's transformation can be witnessed in just under four months. Now, some parts of your growth will happen in an instant. Others will take years. But the frog can remind you that change most often happens in stages. There is a system, a reason, to all things that happen in nature.

What You Will Need
+ Candles for ambient lighting
+ A lighter or matches

+ A piece of paper
+ Some crayons, markers, or colored pencils
+ A green taper candle
+ A small bowl of water
+ *Optional:* firesafe dish

Preparation
Start by lighting your ambient candles. The frog is associated with water and the moon, so you want your space to have that sort of dimly lit feel to it. Give yourself enough light to see, but it should be gentle light.

Instructions
If you haven't done the Personal Growth Meditation listed previously, start by doing it now. If you have done it previously, you can opt to either start with that meditation or reflect on what you learned from it.

When you come back from the meditation, look down at your paper. Begin to draw a frog. Do not worry about making something that would fit in at the Louvre. You are making this frog for you. Use any colors you feel called to use.

When you have your frog, write five qualities you want to bring into your life around the frog. They may be anything you would like, but ideally, they will help you get to the person you want to be when you step into your elder role.

With or without words, say a prayer to the Egyptian frog-headed goddess Heket (or Heqet) asking her to guide your process of change. Then light the candle.

Take your beautifully drawn frog and place it in the bowl of water. Set the bowl in a way that it will reflect the candlelight. As the paper soaks up the water and begins to fall apart, note the process of change that water can create.

You may leave the bowl and the burning candle in a firesafe dish if you will be nearby. Otherwise, extinguish the flame. After the candle has burned out, dispose of the paper and water by composting it so that the process of transformation may continue.

23: Who Am I Meditation

It is common to go through periods of your life when you question who you are and what you know. In truth, you should always be questioning, always asking, and always seeking. I like to think that I am not the same person today that I was yesterday. Experiences, however small or large, have a ripple effect on us at a cellular level. Since our cells vibrate, it makes sense that their frequency can change, thus impacting the frequency of our body as a whole. As you enter into this meditation, do so with an open mind and the willingness to look at yourself through an impartial lens.

Begin Meditation

Get into your usual meditative position. Close your eyes and breathe. In your mind's eye, see a flat, open space. Perhaps it is grassland, beach, or desert. It is vast and open. Now form a lake in your favorite color. That's right, maybe it is a pink lake or an orange lake. Let it form and fill. Step forward to the edge of the lake and stick your left hand into the water. Focus on the feeling in your hand. Does it tingle? Does it feel heightened with energy? Does it have the same resonance as the water, or is it different? Try changing the water color. What happens? Spend a few moments on these questions, then step back from the water and return it to your favorite color.

Now it is time to add plants—your favorite plants. Instinctively, most people will begin with trees. And it is certainly okay to do so. But maybe you have a flower your grandmother used to grow that always makes you think of her. Or perhaps there is a type of bush you saw on a trip to Tahiti that caught your eye. Use these memories as inspiration to fill your space with plants. Touch the plants with your left hand. Energetically, how do they feel?

Most people have a favorite season. And if not, they at least have a preference toward either cold weather or hot weather. Turn the time in this world forward or backward until you reach your favorite season. How does this change the landscape? How does this change the way you feel within your world?

Now that you have water, plant life, and a season, it is time to give your space more dimensions. Think first of your favorite smells. Are they smells that you have always loved? Is there a memory tied to them? Try to sense at least one of your favorite smells wafting in on a breeze. How does that smell interact with the space you have created? How do you feel being surrounded by so many of your favorite things? How does the energy of the smell feel when you breathe it into your body?

Next, think of your favorite sounds. Does your energy tighten? Loosen? Get heightened? Stay the same?

Are there any other favorites you want to add? Time of day? Stones? Animals? Keep going until you feel that your space has enough of your favorites to represent you. When you are done, stand back and look at this world you have created. Does it seem to fit with how you see yourself? Why or why not? Does it feel smooth and cohesive or jagged and rough?

There is no right or wrong answer to these questions. But if your space somehow feels "off" from your whole energetic being, ask yourself why. If it feels like something is missing, then perhaps it is. You do not need to fix these things now. Just make a mental note so that as you work your way through this book, you can notice if and when any changes occur.

24: Journey of Discovery Meditation

In this meditation, you are going to build off of the groundwork you started in the last meditation. You will be returning to the world you previously created in the Who Am I Meditation. This time, though, you will be following a path and are going to discover messages about your life's journey.

Begin Meditation

Start getting into a meditative state and return to the space you created in the previous meditation. You see two paths in front of you: one to the left and one to the right. You see that each of the two paths has smaller trails that connect to it. What you may not see is that the two main paths connect eventually. That means that no matter if you start on the right or the left, you will wind up where you are supposed to be.

Pick a path. Try to go with whichever calls you first, and don't second-guess yourself. Begin walking down the path. Notice the ground beneath your feet. Is it soft? Firm? Smooth? Rocky? Is the path flat, or does it rise and fall?

As you walk, you will begin to see items—animals, places, etc.— that are of personal significance to you, to your past. Keep walking; do not let yourself get distracted by the past, not right now. Keep walking until you come to a cave. It is tucked into a mountain face, and although it is in the wilderness, you know it is quite safe.

As you step inside the cave, you are greeted by a gust of wind. Though you can't see its source, you can tell that the wind is not out of place. You hear the sound of rushing water and climb toward it. You slip through openings and down pathways, searching for the sound.

As you get closer to the water, you find yourself in a large hollow deep within the mountain. There is a golden waterfall cascading into a shimmering pool below. You see someone sitting on a rock with their back to you, and one of their feet is grazing the water. You call out hello, and it echoes through the cave, louder than you would have imagined.

"Come closer," the figure calls to you. Though she hasn't turned, you can sense that she is watching you.

You step closer slowly, not out of fear but out of reverence. When you are close enough to smell her scent—wheat and acorns—she turns around. The goddess Cerridwen looks at you with two white eyes, eyes that see through time and space, eternal eyes. Her wrinkled face forms a smile, and without speaking, she asks you what you seek on your journey.

Answer her with the truth in your heart.

She ponders for a moment and looks deep into your eyes with hers. Then she reaches into the flaming cauldron on her lap. She pulls out something from the ashes and places her closed hand into your palm. She wraps your hand around the item without you seeing it. You know that this is what you need to know to start your journey, the symbol that will guide you on your path toward what you seek.

You open your palm and discover what is inside. You look up to thank the great goddess, but she is gone, leaving no trace of herself in the glittering cave. Any questions you have are left to be answered by you.

As you make your way out of the cave and back down the path, you internalize the meaning or meanings of the item you have been given. Make your way back to the lake where you started. In future visits, you can walk down other trails. But for now, it is time to return to the physical world. Do so as you normally would, slowly returning to your consciousness.

If possible, draw or create a representation of the symbol you were given so that it can serve as a reminder of the journey you are on.

25: The Fates Spell

The idea that there are divine beings who control destiny, or fate, is a widespread concept. In ancient Greece, they were the three Moirai; in Rome, the Parcae. They were known as the Norns in Scandinavia and the Rozhanitsy in Slavic mythology.

This spell will allow you to meet with the Fates and gain knowledge of your destiny. It is particularly helpful if you are at an intersection of life where you feel you need to progress but you are not sure how. It is polite to bring a gift for each of the Fates, especially if you are seeking their favor. For this spell, I will use the Moirai, but it could be adapted to work with any of the embodiments of the Fates.

What You Will Need
+ Biodegradable gifts, one for each Fate
+ Yarn made of natural material, cut into three pieces, each 12–18" long
+ A safety pin
+ A pillow or similar to affix the pins to

Preparation
Lay out your yarn in front of you. Put the safety pin through one end of the threads. Attach the safety pin to a pillow or your jeans, something to hold it in place.

Instructions

Take the first piece of yarn and hold it in your hand. Close your eyes and mentally call to Clotho, the one who spins our thread. She is the one who gives life force. Think about your life and the pivotal moments that have occurred within it. Focus on each and listen for Clotho's words. What does she say?

Now take the second piece of yarn, close your eyes again, and mentally call to Lachesis. She determines the length of the thread and the lifespan of humans and gods. She also has a hand in the things that have not yet happened. Think about what you would like your life to be like and listen for her answers. She is the one who can tell you what is in store for your life.

Atropos is the oldest of the Fates. And though she represents death, she should be approached without fear and, instead, with reverence. Do not query into the when and how of your end, lest she tell you, but only ask that you have a chance to complete all you have come here to do and to die well. Just like with the others, call out to her while holding the third piece of yarn. Think about the balance of life and death, how they are both necessary and natural. Listen to any messages she has for you.

Now weave the three pieces of yarn together while chanting,

> *Clotho who spins,*
> *Lachesis who lengthens,*
> *Atropos who is there at the end,*
> *Weavers, weavers of the web.*
> *Fates of future, present, and past,*
> *Guide my destiny and guide it well.*
> *Guide my life; long may it last.*

Repeat this until you have braided together all of the yarn.

Coil the yarn, sticking the three gifts within it or next to it if they can't be wrapped. Place one at the beginning, one at the middle, and one at the end. Find a place in nature to bury this bundle. As you lay it in the earth, thank the Fates for all they have given to you: abundance, struggle, mirth, and meagerness. All these things are important to creating the whole human being we are.

26: Masks We Wear Spell

Take a moment to consider the various aspects of your personality that you have within you. You are a different version of yourself when you are with your parents vs. with a lover vs. at a PTA meeting. They are all you, but they are select sides of yourself. Masks get a bad rap. Sometimes we need to put one on for survival or to make situations less awkward. One type of mask is a glamour, but there are others. If you find yourself in need of a mask, especially in a public situation, you can use this quick spell. It is recommended that you practice it beforehand so that when you need it, it is there.

What You Will Need
- ✦ Paper
- ✦ Scissors
- ✦ Pens, pencils, markers, or crayons in various colors
- ✦ A mirror
- ✦ *Optional:* string that's long enough to tie around your head

Preparation
Before you begin, think of a situation you were in recently where you wish you could've worn a mask. Maybe you wanted to be braver in a situation where you were scared. Or maybe you wanted to be more

tactful in a recent encounter with a coworker. Perhaps you even wanted to be able to show more emotion. Whatever it is, think about what these characteristics look like.

Instructions

When you have decided what characteristics your mask will have, use your paper and drawing materials to create it. You can use a solid color, make a superhero, do designs, or whatever feels right. It doesn't have to be a work of art. This spell is about tapping into those characteristics and creating visual reminders and cues so you can call on them when you need them.

When you create this mask, put it over your face and look in the mirror. Now take it off. What differences did you see? Practice putting it on and taking it off a few times. Then put the mask to the side and, using your mind's eye, visualize the mask coming on and off your face while saying,

> *When I need you, I have you.*
> *When I call you, you come.*
> *For you are me, and I am you,*
> *And we are connected.*

When you can do that successfully, try it without the mirror and repeat,

> *When I need you, I have you.*
> *When I call you, you come.*
> *For you are me, and I am you,*
> *And we are connected.*

Now you can pull up that mask image in your mind's eye anytime you need it. Though not as long-lasting as a full glamour, it is quite effective. Repeat the process to make different masks for different sets of characteristics you want to keep handy.

27: Glamour Spell

Glamours are misunderstood. It is only in Hollywood where hair color can change instantly with some magic words. (Wouldn't that be nice? It would save me a fortune at the salon.) What they *can* do, though, is help you bring out a hidden aspect of yourself. Glamours help you choose what aspect of self you show to the world through body language, words, tone, and even the energy you give off. Think about it this way: Let's say you are nervous to give a speech. You perform a glamour ... See yourself giving the speech, hearing the applause. You may still be nervous, but no one can tell. This is the illusion. Though it is an illusion, it still comes from a real place.

First, you have to know what you want. Take some time to pinpoint the word you want to use. You may say that you want to appear confident, but if this borders on egotistical, it will not work in your favor. My suggestion is that you start with a word, then go to your handy thesaurus and go through the synonyms. Read a definition for each until you find exactly what you want to portray. This will be the goal of your glamour.

What You Will Need
+ A word that you want to focus on

Preparation
Now, there are several ways to create a glamour. But the one I will give you here will be similar in construction to some of the shielding exercises in the protection chapter. Now is a good time to review them.

This works best if you can be skyclad, but this is not required.

Instructions

You will start off standing in a quiet place, with legs shoulder-width apart and arms down but not touching the rest of your body. Take three slow, deep breaths.

In and out.

In and out.

In and out.

Close your eyes and notice your feet. Notice how they feel on the floor. Are your feet warm? Cold? What about the floor? Is it soft? Hard? Is there texture? Notice all you can about it. When you are ready, and still with your eyes closed, look down at your feet and use your senses to make the ground into grass. Can you smell it? See it? Feel it? Does it tickle your ankles? Wiggle your toes; can you feel it between them?

Take another deep breath in. Listen for the sounds around you... birds, wind, and most importantly, the sound of a waterfall nearby. Make your way to this waterfall.

When you get to this waterfall, you notice this is no ordinary waterfall. It is not water at all. It is liquid silver light flowing down. Before you step into it, say the word "confidence" into the waterfall. The light will change in color, style, or words. Try now the word "timid." What happens to the water?

Give the water a moment to go back to its original state, then step into the pool. Say your word, then step into the falls. Feel and see the light flow over you and through your body. It gathers by your feet and starts to spin. Forming an orb, it surrounds your body, starting at your feet and working its way up to your knees and abdomen, neck, and finally your head. It surrounds you in an orb made of the attribute you wish to portray. When you are completely surrounded, say with authority, "I am [word you used]" three times.

You may now step out of the pool. Focus on the grass and let it slowly turn back into the floor of the room you are in. Breathe deeply and bring your consciousness back to the earthly plane. When you are back, slowly open your eyes. You may now go about your day knowing that this orb surrounds you. How long it lasts depends on how well you were able to visualize it. But it is meant to be temporary. It cannot make you something you are not, but it can highlight traits within yourself that might otherwise stay hidden.

If you need to remove your glamour before it dissolves on its own, you can command it to dissipate and put your hands or feet in the earth or water. Allow the orb that surrounded you to disappear back into the ground.

As you practice this and get better at it, you will be able to do this almost anywhere. You will also be able to keep it for longer periods and customize it to suit your needs and preferences.

Ring-Pass-Not

A *Ring-Pass-Not* is a spiritual barrier that is difficult for us to pass. It may be something we work on throughout multiple lives, or we may pass it in one. But it is an obstacle that is not easy to pass, and once you pass, it will cause a shift in your perception. Your Ring-Pass-Not may be not speaking up for yourself, for example. In this scenario, you may find yourself thinking, I really should have said something, but each time you try, your voice feels held in place, unable to leave.

Think of the Ring-Pass-Not as a cap on a bottle. You can climb to the top of that bottle, but until you remove that cap, you are constrained to what is within that bottle. This is a spell you will most likely need to repeat several times. I have broken it down into three parts. First, discovering what it is. Second, overcoming it. And third, climbing out of the bottle. Part one should be completed a few times on its own before attempting parts two or three.

28: Ring-Pass-Not Part 1: Identification

For this spell, you will call on the Norse god of wisdom and knowledge, Mimir. In Norse mythology, he was decapitated by the Vanir (see glossary). When his head was returned to Odin (head of the Aesir), Odin preserved it with herbs and used to talk to it to gain knowledge. In another variation of the myth, he is associated with Mimir's Well, where Odin drank to receive sacred knowledge.[6]

What You Will Need

- A cup or goblet that is dark on the inside, preferably black
- A cup of spring or well water (Make sure it is safe to drink or buy some.)
- A dark-colored votive candle
- A circle, like an armband or bracelet, made of natural materials and that you are fine with destroying (It should be breakable with a hammer for part 2.)
- An offering of honey
- An offering of bread
- An offering of wine, mead, or juice
- Lighter or matches
- A drum (Alternatively, you can drum on your leg.)

---

6. "Mimir," Encyclopedia Britannica, November 18, 2022, https://www .britannica.com/topic/Mimir.

Preparation

Start by filling the cup with water and placing it in front of the candle. Take the bracelet and slide it over the candle so it rests at the base. Set up the offerings off to the side.

Instructions

Light the candle. Begin to drum while you chant Mimir's name. Start slow and soft.

Repeat his name. Try to use your voice of power (see chapter 4). Find your primal voice. Call Mimir. Ask him to join you. Let the beats of the drum take you into another world. If you feel like dancing, do so. If you feel like stomping your feet, then do that.

> *Mimir,*
> *Your knowledge I seek.*
> *My Ring-Pass-Not*
> *Reveal to me.*

Look into the cup (Mimir's Well). What do you see? You may see something right away; you may not. Slide the bracelet slowly up the candle until you see or get a sense of what your Ring-Pass-Not may be. The answer may come through your intuitive senses. If you need to, repeat the chant.

When you have an idea of what your Ring-Pass-Not is, slide the bracelet off of the candle and put it on. Then approach your offerings. Put a generous amount of honey on the bread and pour a generous amount of drink into the cup. After the candle burns down, present these after sunset to Mimir as a thank-you for his wisdom.

29: Ring-Pass-Not Part 2: Overcoming

Now that you know what your Ring-Pass-Not is, it is time to work on overcoming it. For this part of the spell, you will want to wear your bracelet every day for two weeks. You will be working with the Norse god Thor, as he is an expert in overcoming obstacles.

What You Will Need

- Acacia oil
- The bracelet or armband you used in the previous part of the spell
- A journal and pen
- A hammer
- A jar
- An offering of mead and bread

Preparation

None.

Instructions

Each morning, put nine drops of acacia oil onto your bracelet. As you do, close your eyes and ask Thor for strength. Wear the bracelet everywhere you go (or carry it if you can't wear it). Put down your phone and pay attention to the world around you. There will be moments and opportunities to take the next step toward breaking through your Ring-Pass-Not.

Each night, when you get home, record these moments. How did you interact with them? Did you move forward even though you were afraid? Did you not? Try not to judge your actions; just notice if you were held in place (figuratively) or not and why you think that is. For example, if your Ring-Pass-Not is never taking opportunities because you fear you will fail (or succeed), you might see an ad for a job you would love. Did you apply, or did you tell yourself you wouldn't get it anyway?

At the end of two weeks, look at your journal. Did you take any steps to break through? Even one is a success. But the more times you do it, the better.

Take your bracelet to a place outside and set it against a rock. You are going to swing the hammer, so make sure that you are not working on a delicate surface. Before you strike, you will ask Thor to embue your hammer with the strength of his hammer, Mjölnir (rhymes with *mule deer*).

> *Mighty Thor,*
> *Thunderous One.*
> *As Mjölnir swings,*
> *That which blocks me is undone.*

Strike the bracelet. Strike it with all your might. See the barriers that block you dissolve with each blow.

Repeat the phrase and strike it again. Do this until there are at least four pieces of bracelet around you. Collect the pieces, especially the big ones, and put them in a jar. You will use them for the next part of the spell. Leave the offering for Thor.

Over the next few days, keep watching for opportunities. Do you take them? Or do you let fear hold you in place?

30: Ring-Pass-Not Part 3: Climbing Out

Next, you must climb through your Ring-Pass-Not and grow something in its place. The Norse goddess Idunn oversees rejuvenation and spring. Her apples helped the gods stay youthful. For you, the seeds from apples will create new opportunities and beginnings to replace your Ring-Pass-Not.

What You Will Need

- The jar with the bracelet or armband pieces you used in the previous part of the spell
- A cloth
- An offering of honey, bread, and white wine or cider
- 9 apple seeds
- 9 scoops of dirt (They can be small if your jar is small.)

Preparation

None.

Instructions

Pull out the pieces of the bracelet and lay them on the cloth. Breathe with intention and consider for a moment all that you have had happen in the past few weeks. Ask yourself if you feel as if you have broken through your Ring-Pass-Not. Ask yourself if there is some part of yourself that feels more awakened, more alive.

Dab a bit of honey on the bracelet. Then do the same with the wine. Say, "For Idunn, these offerings made."

Pick up the seeds: "For my future, I plant intention."

Pick up the jar: "For opportunities to flourish."

Place the first scoop of dirt in the jar. Place a piece of the bracelet on top of the dirt and one seed. "One scoop to be the beginning."

Place two more scoops of dirt in the jar. Place another piece of the bracelet on top of the dirt and two more seeds. "Three scoops for the zest of life."

Place three more scoops of dirt in the jar. Place another piece of the bracelet on top of the dirt and three more seeds. "Six scoops to nurture my potential."

Place two more scoops of dirt in the jar. Place the remaining pieces of the bracelet on top of the dirt and three more seeds. Then cover them with your last scoop of dirt and say, "Nine scoops for wisdom I have gained."

After the jar is filled, bury it in your backyard. If this is not possible, dig a hole, dump out dirt, bracelet, and seeds, and cover the hole back up. Then recycle the jar.

Leave the offering for Idunn.

Chapter 4
Empowerment

B ecoming an empowered human being should be on everybody's spiritual growth checklist. Empowerment, in this case, simply means being able to step into your innate power. Every one of you has personal power woven into your very DNA. Now, you may be in a home or work situation where you do not feel like this is true. I've been there. So believe me when I tell you that you still can access your power. This will be harder for some of you than it will be for others. But just keep at it.

For a long time, I gave away my power. I gave it away to relationships with insignificant people; I gave it away to drugs, to strangers, to everybody. Back then, I did not see the power that I held. Now that I do, I want to help you see your power. This starts with honesty toward yourself and others. A simple concept, but so very hard to put into practice. This process began in chapter 3. Now I want you to begin to understand what it means to be you. There is knowing who you are, then there is owning who you are. And while much overlap exists between the two, they are each worth exploring as their own idea and concept. Let us begin.

31: Soul Voice Journey

Our soul voice does not speak in any human language. It speaks the same language as the universe: vibrations, patterns, and intuition. It speaks the language of energy. Think about a time when you didn't want to do something, and I don't mean laundry or taking out the trash. I'm talking about a life situation where you felt that what you were about to do conflicted with some aspect of yourself. Maybe it was being pressured into bullying someone or stealing or engaging in sexual acts you didn't want to. That feeling you had was your soul voice letting you know that this was not in alignment with who you are.

Your soul voice is talking all the time, trying to guide you down the path that matches your vibration. It is often quiet, but it can be loud when you are on the right track. Now think of a time when you were doing something you love to do. Maybe you were playing an instrument, riding a horse, painting, or playing soccer. Whatever it was, think about that feeling that resonated through you. This was also your soul voice speaking. Still noticeable, still loud, but with a much more pleasing resonance. This meditation will help you learn to listen to your soul voice and acknowledge the wisdom it has to impart.

What You Will Need

+ At least 4 candles for illumination (Size and color don't matter.)
+ Matches or a lighter

Preparation

Get comfortable and light the candles. If possible, light a circle of them around you. This meditation works best when you are wearing comfy clothes or skyclad. Be barefoot or wear socks made out of a natural material.

Instructions

This journey will require you to sit, at least for a moment, and ask yourself, What do I really need? Before you answer, let that deeper part of yourself answer. As humans, we tend to have prepared answers— not just that we give to other people, but ones we give to ourselves. From a young age, we are taught that we are supposed to want certain things. As we grow, part of us grows accustomed to this expectation. So as you meditate, wait for the answer.

Let your breath get deep. Let it guide you into your body, below your skin. Feel the area where your skin connects to muscle, your hypodermis. Ask yourself the question, What do I need? either silently or out loud, but this time, let your feet answer. What do they tell you? Your soul voice is in every part of you, from your toenails to the tips of your hair. Each of your feet may give you a different answer, or they may say the same thing. Either way, make a mental note before moving on.

Move up your body slowly, repeating the process of asking and listening. Go from your feet to your legs to your hips to your heart and chest to your arms, fingertips, throat, and mind. The more individual parts you ask, the more in-depth your meditation will be. Each time, be patient and wait for that part of you to answer the question, What do I need? Anything you can provide to that area while in meditation, do so.

Now think about some aspects of your life: job, where you live, something that has been on your mind. Pick an aspect and ask each part of your body what it feels about that aspect. Do your feet like where you live? How is your stomach impacted by your job?

When you come out of your meditation, follow through by providing anything you can to your body that it asked for. Maybe your hands need a massage, for example.

As you go through your days, your weeks, your months, check in with these parts of yourself. If you are about to take a job in a new city, ask your toes what they think of the idea. You may find that all your parts shout joyously in agreement. You may find they don't. But by checking in, you are learning how your world and your choices impact your physical being.

32: Voice of Power (Casting Voice) Spell

Your voice of power is slightly different than your soul voice. Where your soul voice is something that speaks to you, your voice of power is the voice you use to speak back, to manifest, to create action and change. This is not a scream, nor is it your loudest voice. You might not even need to raise your voice above speaking level. Your voice of power carries authority. It is matter-of-fact, neither cruel nor meek.

Once you find this voice, it is what you will use when you cast circle, when you command, when you manifest words into reality. It may take you a few tries to get it, but once you do, you will feel empowered and in control whenever you use it. You will use your voice of power for many of the spells and rituals in this book.

What You Will Need
+ This spell requires no tools

Preparation
Go to the working space you have created. Close the door and, if possible, remove all sounds from the room. This is a perfect time to send your significant other to the movies with the kids.

Instructions

It is best to start with a power word, such as "no." In your softest whisper, say "no." What happened? Did your body vibrate? This time, say it louder. Once again, ask yourself if you felt it in your body. Repeat this until you reach a level that feels like you could be heard in a room.

Now let's work on the vibration. You are looking for a vibration that is commanding but not cruel. Think about a time when your dog was about to make a mess on the carpet, for example, and you told them "no" in a way that got them to stop. That is the level of command you are looking for. Once you find it, you can learn to use your voice of power in little more than a whisper. But first, you have to find it.

If you can home in on a moment, such as with the dog, this will help you find your voice of power. If not, say "no" casually in the volume you have already established. Then raise and lower the tone until you reach your voice of power. You should be able to feel it resonate in your core.

Once you find it, practice different words such as, "command," "yes," "stop," and "now." Remember, the point of the casting voice is not to be rude, but simply to command. This voice will be used in other spells and rituals throughout the book.

33: Reminder to Speak Spell

This is another excellent spell that was designed and written by my good friend and ordained priestess JoyBelle Phelan. It is the second of five that you'll find in the book.

Your voice matters! This spell is to remind you that you matter and that your voice needs to be shared. Each of us has a unique story, and a balanced throat chakra can enable and empower that very sharing.

You will be accessing deities that support communication. The Greek goddess Iris is not only associated with the rainbow but also communication and messages. In association with his role as a god who can easily cross boundaries, Greek Hermes is prominently worshiped as a messenger, often described as the messenger of the gods since he can convey messages between the divine realms and the world of mortals.

What You Will Need

+ 1 of the following stones: blue lace agate, blue chalcedony, celestite, sodalite, or lapis lazuli

Preparation

The throat chakra is where we will be focusing. It is located at the base of your neck, responsible for the communication and expression of your thoughts and feelings. The mantra for this chakra is "I speak."

Before you begin, choose a mantra to include in this work. Some suggestions are:

+ "I live and speak my truth."
+ "I communicate clearly."
+ "I know when to speak and when to listen."
+ "I advocate for myself, and I stand up for what I believe."

Instructions

Create safe space, as directed in chapter 1.

Ask Iris and Hermes to join you. You can simply say, "Iris, Hermes, I ask you here now to aid my work."

Hold your chosen stone in your hand. Speak aloud the mantra you have chosen three times. As you do, know that you are imbuing your charm with the confidence, energy, and determination to speak your truth aloud.

Carry your charm and use it whenever you need a reminder to speak!

Senses of Power Spells

You can use these variations of the Voice of Power Spell to find your power by utilizing your other senses. For any number of reasons, you may prefer to not use your voice of power or may want to use your other senses to add dimension to your voice of power. The following spells will take you through each of your senses to find the power that can be harnessed. It should be noted that the power is yours. In each of these spells, it is not the item giving you power. You already have the power. These are simply methods for helping bring it out.

34: Scent of Power Spell

There is a link between your sense of smell and your brain functioning and mood. When you are finding your scent of power, you will be looking for a scent that seems to uplift your whole body. You may have to perform this spell several times before you find it, and you may have more than one.

What You Will Need
+ 3 essential oils that appeal to you (I recommend bergamot, rosemary, and lemongrass.)
+ 1 taper candle in your favorite color
+ Lighter or matches

Preparation

One by one, waft the smell from the essential oil bottle to your nose. Resist the urge to put the bottle up to your nose directly, as this can alter your impression of the oils and can temporarily stun your membrane.

Instructions

Smell each one. Which one makes your body vibrate? What happens if you combine two or three of the oils? When you find a scent that makes you feel powerful, you can use this to help you in spellwork by anointing a candle to use now or for later. When you are out in the world and want to utilize your scent of power, you can do so by dabbing some on your skin. This is especially powerful for those quick, at-work spells like giving yourself courage during a presentation.

35: Taste of Power Spell

Taste and smell are linked. But that doesn't mean that you can't utilize the power of taste on its own. Think about a morning cup of coffee or tea, when you savor that first sip and it mentally prepares you for the day. This is the same idea. But instead, you are going to think about foods and flavors that resonate with you. (Maybe you love bananas or celery sticks coated in peanut butter.)

This works best if you stick with natural flavors. Do not ingest anything that is not edible.

What You Will Need

+ 3–5 simple foods that you enjoy, for example, vanilla ice cream, black tea, dark chocolate
+ A glass of water to drink

Preparation

If your foods need to be cooked or frozen for them to be edible, do this beforehand. Try to avoid seasoning or sweetening your food. You want to experience the taste of each item on its own.

Instructions

One by one, taste each item and savor them. As they sit on your tongue, do they give you a feeling of power? Contentment? Focus? Between eating each food, drink some water to cleanse your palate. Once you find the one that resonates with your energetic self, you can use it by keeping the flavor accessible. Maybe it is purple grapes kept in the fridge that will allow you to be the best version of yourself when you need it.

36: Sound of Power Spell

Have you ever heard a song and felt it flow throughout your whole body? That is the idea behind the sound of power. However, instead of being a song that is your favorite, you want a sound that will awaken every sound in your body. This can be music, but it doesn't have to be. For me, the draw of a bow over a violin sends waves of power through my body. I feel like I can tackle the world when the right music is playing in my ears. This is what you are striving for. If the sound of lightning crashing in the sky gives you this feeling, then use it.

What You Will Need

- ◆ 3–5 songs or sounds
- ◆ A way to play them

Preparation

To begin, put your songs or sounds on a playlist. If you are playing a drum or instrument, have this accessible in your space. If you are using something electric to play your song or sounds, try to have your playlist set up with white noise in between each.

Instructions

Put on the first sound. As you listen to it, try to be present in the moment of that sound. Can you feel it in your core? Does it vibrate in your body? Do you feel powerful as you listen? If not, what do you feel?

Repeat this with each sound, one at a time. Leave some moments of silence in between each one so your body has time to reset. When you find your sound of power, keep it in your musical library so it is accessible.

It should be noted that there might be an element of a particular song or sound that lends you power, such as violins in my example above or perhaps a particular bass line. It is possible, then, to make a whole power playlist and listen to it when you need that oomph.

37: Touch of Power Spell

Something to know about touch is that the objects we touch aren't really solid. They are a mass of vibrating, tightly packed atoms. I will spare you the physics lecture, but if you can bear this in mind, you will understand that everything you touch has a vibration. Hot water vibrates differently than cold. Soft items carry a different vibration than firm items. Some of these differences are so nuanced that it can be hard to tell, especially when you add in the history of an item. You are looking for items with an energy that leaves you feeling empowered either by wearing or touching them.

What You Will Need
+ 3–5 items of different ages and textures

Preparation
Just as you have done with the other senses, you'll want to gather some items you are drawn to. Place these around you, within arm's reach. If you are using clothing, you can put it on if you would like. If you are touching non-wearable items, touch them with an open palm.

Instructions
One by one, hover your hand close to, but not touching, each item, and see how it feels. Go beyond the texture and warmth: How does the energy feel? Now touch the item or put it on. How does it feel to wear it? Have it in your hand? Imagine yourself in a situation where you need extra power. Does this item provide it? When you find your power item, you can wear it or hold it as it is, or specifically designate it as a power item.

38: Vision of Power Spell

For most of us, vision is how we get our information about the world. But vision is not just what we see with our physical eyes; it also happens to be what we see in our mind's eye. Your vision of power is about what your inner eye finds appealing and empowering.

What You Will Need
+ A full-length mirror
+ 3–5 items of clothing with different colors and patterns
+ 3–5 household items with different colors and patterns

Preparation

Set up your full-length mirror in your working space. Gather all of your items together so that they are easily accessible.

Instructions

One by one, either put the item on or hold it in front of your body while facing the mirror. If you can see your aura, notice how it changes the color or vibration. If you are not adept at this skill, you can try to sense how it changes your cells or your energy field.

When you find an item that calls out your power, set it aside. Stand again in front of the mirror and visualize that item being wrapped around you. Anytime you need to call forward this energy, visualize it. Know that it is there, and in essence, it will be.

39: Step Into Your Power Meditation

After you do the Senses of Power workings, move to this next exercise to ensure that you can access your power whenever it is needed. So even if you left your essential oil of power at home, you can still tune in to it. Pick at least one of the senses from the Senses of Power spells. You can use more if you would like.

Begin Meditation

Close your eyes and breathe deeply, intentionally, a few times.

Whatever sense you have chosen to work with, try to have it fill you up. As you breathe, let the scent, taste, sound, touch, or image fill every cell of your body. If it helps to visualize a color filling you up, do so. When you become practiced at this, you will even be able to pick up on the change in your cellular vibration.

Once the sensation has filled you, toes to head, slowly open your eyes and repeat, "I am power. Power is me" nine times or until you feel empowered.

40: Own Your Air Journey

Thoughts have power, the power of air. Ideally, you want to own your thoughts and not let them own you. But, for so many of us, the constant assault of self-talk and societal expectations makes us question if our thoughts are even truly our own. When you feel the cacophony of messages barraging you, then use this spell to restore your thoughts.

What You Will Need

+ Binaural beats or instrumental music (I like Ludovico Einaudi, but anything that you can feel in your body when you listen to it will work.)
+ Phone, laptop, tablet, or another device to play music on
+ *Optional*: headphones

Preparation

Start by taking five deep breaths. Set up your music and press play.

Instructions

Sit in your space and tune in to the music. Let it embrace you. Is it slow and patient or rapid and short? As you let the music wash over you, begin to let your thoughts come in. Imagine you are guarding a door, and you get to choose how many thoughts come into this musical world and which ones.

"No, thought. Not you," you say to one.

"You may enter," you say to another.

When you let a thought in, let it dance with the notes of the music. Does it transform? If so, how? Let the thought float and flow until it is your thought. Only you will know when this happens, but a good indicator is when it stops changing or when it feels true. Let this thought drift away as you let in another and repeat the process.

You can use this with one thought or five or twenty; it is up to you. The important thing is to have your thoughts be yours. A more complex version of this meditation can have you examine thoughts that stem from childhood and young adult interactions. The process is the same. Both are clearing.

41: Own Your Fire Spell

When most people think of fire, they think of a raging forest fire, but fire is also the flame that cooks our food. It is the warmth of the glowing embers in the hearth. It is passion and the force that burns away the old to make room for the new. As you enter into this spell, think about what you no longer need and which passions need to be rekindled. You cannot welcome in the new unless you clear away the old.

What You Will Need
  + An orange pillar candle
  + Firesafe bowl
  + Lighter or matches
  + 2 bay leaves
  + Fine-tip marker in a dark color

Preparation
This spell asks you to give up something—an attribute that you no longer need. Spend some time selecting a trait you are willing to part

with before you begin. Then summarize it into no more than two words. You will need to know the word(s) as you begin your spell.

Place your candle in the firesafe container.

Instructions

Light your candle.

On the underside of one bay leaf, write the word(s) that represent what you are willing to part with.

Hold your nondominant hand near the candle flame. Hold it close enough that you can feel its warmth on your palm but not close enough to burn your skin. A blue light fills you to draw out that which is no longer needed. Use the candle to light the leaf and put it in the firesafe bowl. Let it burn.

On the other bay leaf, on the top this time, write in what area of your life you want to increase your passion.

Now put up your dominant hand to the flame, once again holding it just close enough to feel the heat. Imagine the flame filling you with orange light. This is the new. This is what you are welcoming, what you have just made room for.

When you are filled with the orange light, use the candle to light your bay leaf and let it burn in the bowl. Let the candle burn down. After it does, scatter the ashes of the bay leaves outside your home in each of the four cardinal directions.

42: Own Your Water Spell

Water, by its very nature, is cleansing. After a fresh rain, particularly one that is long and nourishing, the world becomes new, as if all was washed away and forgiven. Water is linked to emotions. When we cry, we are releasing emotions that have been stored in our cells. We reset, we cleanse, we renew. In this spell, you will own the ebb and flow of the water that lives within. You will begin to acknowledge the range of your emotions and learn how to cleanse them. You will begin to feel your emotions but learn to not let them control you.

What You Will Need
+ A bottle of rainwater (You can alternatively use a bottle of river, stream, or creek water.)
+ A bowl
+ 3 strips of water-soluble paper
+ A marker

Preparation
Before you begin, prepare your bowl of water. It doesn't need to be full, but there should be enough for the tips of your fingers to be submerged.

Instructions
Get comfortable and close your eyes for a moment. As you breathe in and out, think about a few emotions you're feeling or have recently felt. Pick one, two, or three to begin with, and write each emotion on one of the strips of paper. Take the first one and hold it in your fingers. Let this emotion fill you up. It might get uncomfortable, but that's okay. Do not shy away from this emotion. Hold this emotion for a few moments. If your body tries to laugh or cry or shake, let it.

Now hold this same piece of paper between the palms of your hands. Will all the emotion you just felt to go into the paper while saying, "[Emotion], I feel you, but you do not control me."

Put the paper into the bowl of water with your fingertips. Let any residual emotion flow into the water as you hold your fingertips there.

When you feel ready, take the second piece of paper and repeat the process. Then repeat the process with the third. If, after you complete one or two, you do not wish to continue with the other slips of paper, that is all right. You can put them aside and attempt the spell again later when you feel able.

The paper will begin to disintegrate in the bowl of water—sometimes in minutes, and sometimes it will take longer. You may leave the papers to disintegrate. When they are done, dispose of them in an eco-conscious manner, such as composting.

43: Own Your Earth Spell

This spell will help you get comfortable in your body and learn to appreciate its physical, earthy form. We avoid discomfort and pain—those are givens—but how many of us are comfortable within our own skin? Owning your earth is owning your physical form. You are as beautiful and unique as anything in nature. Think about a rock that has been compressed, stressed, broken, and windblown. It may have a rough surface, some cracks, and spots where minerals blended, but it is that much more appealing because of its quirks. You, too, have been stretched, stressed, shaped, and blended, and that is why you are so stunning.

What You Will Need
+ 4 stones that represent your physical being
+ A mirror
+ *Optional:* a bowl of earth, preferably from a garden or park space

Preparation

Do this spell barefoot. If possible, do this spell outside in a natural space. If that is not possible, bring some plants into your space while you do this ritual. You can opt to use dirt from the space you're in if you're outside, rather than the bowl of dirt.

Instructions

Pick up one of the rocks that you have chosen. Roll it around between your fingers. Why did you choose this rock? How does it represent you? Hold up the mirror with one hand and the rock next to your face with the other. See how you are made of the same earth that this stone is. Hold this stone and admire its qualities. See its qualities within you.

Repeat this with each of the four stones.

Now hold two stones in each hand, trying to balance equal weight, and place your feet on the earth below you. If you are inside while doing this ritual, touch your bowl of earth with your bare feet.

Close your eyes. Feel the earth beneath you. Can you feel Mother Earth's heartbeat? Feel the earth that you hold in your hand. Feel the earth that is your body.

Think about all the parts of your body. See each part as part of the rocks you hold in your hands. Are your toes granite? Are your eyes obsidian? Was your stomach formed in volcanic pressure or in the sea? Let these rock images of your body fill your mind. Take your time. When you feel like you have spent time with your body in its earth form, you may take a deep breath in and out and shake your body a bit at a time. As you visualize the pieces of your earth self falling to the floor, consider if your understanding of your body, your appreciation for it, has changed at all.

Repeat this spell as often as you like. When you look at yourself in the mirror, instead of saying things like, "I wish my [blank] was [blankier]," try, "Look at that lovely piece of igneous rock." Bit by bit, the ability to love your body will come to you.

44: Own Your Power Spell

Now that you have done the work to get to know each element, you will combine them in this spell. All of these elements exist within you. Even if you haven't done the owning your element spells listed previously, you can still use this one to get your power in balance.

What You Will Need

+ *Earth:* a bowl of dirt
+ *Air:* lavender incense
+ *Fire:* a yellow taper or chime candle
+ *Water:* a cup of water
+ Lighter or matches

Preparation

Set up the four elemental representations around you. Put the bowl of dirt in the north, the incense in the east, the candle in the south, and the cup of water in the west. Light the candle and incense. Sit in the middle of the elements.

Instructions

Touch each element (except fire—just get close enough to feel its heat). As you do, say the corresponding part: "I am earth. Tangible, physical, and real." (×3)

As you chant, visualize a green light coming from the bowl of earth into your hand and filling your body: "I am air, sovereign of my thoughts." (×3)

As you chant, visualize a soft yellow light coming from the incense smoke into your hand and filling your body: "I am fire, full of passions, changeable." (×3)

As you chant, visualize a red light coming from the candle flame into your hand and filling your body: "I am water, cleansed and renewed." (×3)

As you chant, visualize a blue light coming from the bowl of water into your hand and filling your body.

Now see these colors swirling within your body and say, "I am earth, I am air, I am fire, I am water, I am the universe. I am all things. And all things are me."

See and meditate on the meaning of all these parts. When you are done, let the candle burn down, then dispose of each element by returning it to where it goes. If you are keeping a magical journal, you can write down the experience.

45: Empowerment Chant

It is not always possible to stop and do a whole spell or meditation. If you need a bit of empowerment while you're out and about in the world, you can repeat this chant either out loud or to yourself.

What You Will Need
+ No items are needed

Preparation
If you are saying this chant out loud, take yourself to a place where you feel comfortable chanting, maybe a bathroom or your car. If you

are in a place where you can't say the words out loud, you can repeat them in your head.

Instructions
Stand or sit comfortably. Say,

> *I am the sand.*
> *I am the sky.*
> *I am fire.*
> *I am rain.*
> *I am all things.*
> *All things are me.*
> *I am connected.*
> *All things are we.*

Repeat it until you feel strengthened and connected.

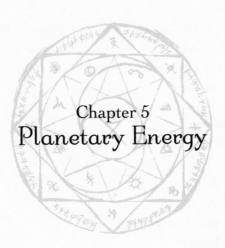

Chapter 5
Planetary Energy

The influence of the planets on our lives—their movements, their placements, and their roles in the universe—has intrigued humans since we first looked up at the sky. This section is going to help you tap into planetary energy and use it to become empowered by the essence of the celestial body you are working with.

For those of you who have not experienced it yet, the planets each have their own sound. That's right, you can listen to Jupiter. How cool is that? These sounds are available online and for free on sites like NASA.[7] A simple search can have you hearing the healing essence of Venus or the chattiness of Mercury. You can include them with each planetary meditation or not.

Additionally, you will notice that planetary incenses and oils are on your shopping list for many of these spells. If you go to your local metaphysical shops, they will either carry specially made blends, make

---

7. "All Planet Sounds from Space (Recorded by NASA) | Gingerline Media," YouTube video, 8:37, March 28, 2022, https://www.youtube.com/watch ?v=uhGKMh2Bhns.

one for you, or suggest a place where these incenses can be acquired. When all of these options fail, you can substitute any readily accessible herb that corresponds to each planet. Here is a list that can be used for both oils and incenses.

+ *Sun:* Myrrh
+ *Moon:* Mugwort
+ *Mercury:* Mullein
+ *Venus:* Vervain
+ *Earth:* Pine
+ *Mars:* Mustard seed
+ *Jupiter:* Thyme
+ *Saturn:* Patchouli
+ *Uranus:* True unicorn root
+ *Neptune:* Gum benzoin
+ *Pluto:* Sandalwood

46: The Sun Spell

The sun represents strength and power. It is energetic and fervent. Though this spell is best performed on a Sunday, a sunny day, or at either Midwinter or Midsummer, it can be utilized any time you need that fiery, energetic energy in your life. And if you're not shy, it can be performed anywhere.

What You Will Need

+ A song that brings solar energy (Some examples might be salsa music, music that has a strong brass section, or even something that just feels fiery and makes you want to dance. Chaotic binaural beats work well.)

+ A stone to represent the sun: sunstone, ruby, goldstone,
gold (technically a metal), amber, citrine, and calcite
work well

Preparation
Pick a space where you can move around. If you can be outside in
the sunlight, all the better. But it can be inside. You will need to have
a way to play your music.

Instructions
Raise your hands to the sun, turn on the music you have chosen, and
dance. As you dance, call out to the Greek Helios to empower you
with the energy of the sun. You can ask silently or call out with the
full force of your voice of power. Dance and visualize the light of the
sun entering your body. Let it fill you up until your fingertips glow
with bright, golden light.

Pull out the stone you have selected and hold it between your
cupped hands while you move. Send the energy from the sun that is
held in your hands into the stone. Do not worry; the sun's energy is
limitless as far as magical purposes are concerned.

Keep dancing with the stone in hand until you feel energized,
then wind down. The stone can be tucked away in your pocket and
pulled out when you need a bit of the sun's empowerment. This stone
can also be carried when you need to present your most confident self.

47: The Moon Spell
Most people know that the moon ties into our emotional state. What
usually isn't considered is that by understanding the ebb and flow
of our emotional tides, we can be better prepared for the highs and

lows. That's right: We are not helpless victims of our emotions. We can understand them and utilize the strength that is carried in each emotion. Think about sadness. (Don't worry, it's only for a moment.) Sadness exists to help us understand love and happiness and to mourn and to be complex. Happiness exists to help us understand what we like. So, instead of shying away from emotions, we should attempt to understand them in context. That is what moon empowerment is about: knowing our waxes and our wanes and allowing our emotions to empower us.

What You Will Need
+ A moonstone or opal
+ A white taper candle to represent the Greek goddess Selene
+ Matches or a lighter

Preparation
It is preferable to do this spell during the full moon, but as the moon has her shades, so do emotions. Any nighttime hour will, therefore, work. If you can be in a place where you can physically see the moon, it will help.

Instructions
Cast a circle if you normally do so.

Hold the opal or moonstone in your receiving hand. With your palm open, raise your receiving hand to the sky. Using your sending hand, light the candle. See the light of the moon flowing from the sky to your hand and into the stone, down your body, and into the spark of candlelight.

As you light the candle, say, "Selene, Glowing Silvery One, Watcher of the Tides. Join me, guide me, lend me your understanding of the tides within. Hail and welcome."

Pull your moonstone hand down toward your body, and see it bringing the energy of the moon down to your heart. Bring up your other hand so they are both resting roughly over your heart. If you can see the moon, spend a few moments bathing in her light.

In your mind's eye, see the moon as her full-bodied self. Then see her slowly waning a sliver at a time until she gets to her mysterious, dark self. Then see her growing, still slowly, a sliver at a time, until she is back to full.

Repeat this, but next time, see your emotions waning and waxing with her. As they ebb and flow, repeat,

> *Emotions clear,*
> *Emotions known.*
> *All live in me,*
> *My body, their home.*
> *Selene, Selene,*
> *I call to thee.*
> *Selene, Selene,*
> *Let my ebbs and flows*
> *Be known to me.*

Repeat this three times. Then, still visualizing the moon, have her return to a state of fullness. Be present under the moonlight. Hold out the moonstone or opal in your hand. Does it seem different now? If so, how?

Place it at the base of the candle and let the candle burn down. Carry the stone with you, and when you need to honor your emotions, put the stone in your hand and be reminded of the cyclical moon.

48: Mercury Spell

Mercury, both the Roman god and the planet, influences the realm of communication. There are many ways that we humans communicate—most of them nonverbal. This spell can help you tap into your communicative abilities. While it can be used at any time, it is especially effective to use this spell when there is a chance that you could be misunderstood.

What You Will Need
- A nice piece of paper
- A nice pen that writes smoothly
- A firesafe container
- A lighter or matches
- A small bottle you can carry with you

Preparation
Lay your paper out on a flat surface. Have your pen handy.

Instructions
On the top of your paper, draw the Mercury astrological symbol in the upper right corner with your nice pen.

In each of the other three corners, write a word or draw a symbol that represents the type of communication you want to achieve. For example, you might put "clarity" if you want to present a clear message, or "persuasive" if you are trying to persuade someone to see things your way.

In the center of the paper, write the following: "I say what I mean."

Spend a few moments considering the meaning of what you want to say. Then write, "My clarity is universal."

Visualize yourself in a room where everyone understands exactly what you are saying. Write, "My words, my tone, and my voice all convey my message."

Now visualize your intended outcome. What is the end result? Try to see or feel this as clearly as you can.

When the image is clear in your mind, place the paper in the firesafe container and light it. As the smoke wafts from the bowl, look to see if it takes on shapes. Do any of these shapes represent sounds, like a musical note? Do not breathe in the smoke, but try to grab some in your hand and rub it on your throat.

After they cool, bottle some of the ashes. They can be dabbed on when you need to increase your communicative abilities. You don't need a lot of ashes; you can simply place a dab under your clothes or put them in the bottle and tuck it somewhere not visible.

49: Venus Spell

The planet Venus is named after the Roman goddess of love, Venus. But Venus, like so many goddesses of love, doesn't work solely within the realms of romantic love. She also works within the realms of the harder-to-attain loves: love of self, wholeness of being, sensuality, art, sociability, and love of life. In this spell, you will tap into these more elusive aspects of Venus through her planetary energies. This spell works best when it is done in ambient lighting, so either candlelight or dim lighting.

What You Will Need
- Tea roses (ground and loose)
- A teacup
- A saucer
- Boiled water
- A dark red or bloodred votive candle
- Rose essential oil
- Matches or lighter
- *Optional:* extra candles for lighting

Preparation
Have everything set up before you begin. Place the roses in the bottom of the cup. Boil the water. After the water has boiled, remove the water from the heat for a few seconds before pouring it over the tea roses.

Instructions
While the tea is steeping, anoint the candle with rose oil, light it, and say, "Welcome Venus, goddess of all affections and attentions."

After a few minutes, the tea is ready. Grab the cup and hold it so that the candle flame is reflected in the water. Gaze at the flame. Listen for any messages the goddess may have for you.

Say, "I drink in self-love." Take a few sips of the tea. Let the warm liquid be felt as it slides down your throat and into your body.

Slowly and intentionally drink the tea one sip at a time.

With the second sip, say, "I drink in wholeness of being." Just as before, let yourself feel it sliding down your throat and into your body.

With your next sip, say, "I drink in sensuality."

Then: "I drink in art."

"I drink in sociability."

"I drink in love of life."

Each time, the sips should be felt while they enter your body. This process should not be rushed. If you still have tea left, you can add water to it and drink with intentions such as friendship, healing, or universal love.

When all your tea is nearly gone, flip the cup upside down onto the saucer. Let it drain for thirty seconds or so. When you flip the cup back over, you will see a message from Venus in the leaves. Try not to overthink it. Whatever first comes to mind, that is your message. Spend the next minutes or hours reflecting on the meaning of the message. Let the cup sit in front of the candle as it burns down. After the candle has gone out, thank Venus for her presence.

Offer the rose petals to Venus with your gratitude: "Hail and farewell, Venus."

You can make some of this tea whenever you need Venusian energy in your life.

50: Earth Spell

The world we live in is a physical one. We require things to live: food, shelter, transportation, our bodies—all of these things are physical. There is a tendency within metaphysical communities to shun the material world. While we can all probably agree that the acquisition of things to the point of excess doesn't align with our spiritual selves, we should not completely shun all that manifests on the physical plane. We should simply learn how to get our comforts in an eco-conscious way. This spell is about the line between comfort and excess: identifying it, acknowledging it, and making decisions that align with our highest being.

What You Will Need

+ A bowl of dirt
+ A seed

Preparation

For this spell, like most spells, you should be barefoot.

Instructions

Look around the room you are in. Out loud, try to list everything that exists in that room: table, lamp, floors, carpet, chair, altar, candles, etc. List everything you see for five minutes.

Now put your hands in the bowl of earth and close your eyes. Breathe with intention for several minutes. Then try to rename as many items as you can. Do not worry if you miss some (or even most) of them. The important part is that while you're listing, focus on how your hands feel in the bowl of earth. Is there a point when they start to get heavy? Cold? Hot? Pay attention. The earth is telling you if these items align.

Visualize the room in your mind's eye. How does it feel? Is it comfortable? Constraining?

Without leaving your spot, mentally go through the rooms of your home. Do they have an energetic weight to them? If so, is this a heavy weight? Is it light? Does the space need more? Need less? How could you make each space feel balanced? Go through each room in this way, asking these questions.

Now begin to ask your body these questions: What does your physical self need? Are you getting it? If not, how can you advocate for yourself to get this physical need met? Think about the shoes you normally wear. Are they adequate? Think about your clothing. Does it protect you from the elements? Is it in good condition? Have you been buying more than you need? Have you been avoiding buying new items even though yours are in unsatisfactory condition?

When you come out of the meditation, slowly bring your hands out of the bowl of dirt. Look around at your room with new eyes. What have you discovered? Are you aligned with your earth? Are you providing yourself with what you need? Without excess? Without lacking?

For the next few weeks, make an effort to slowly get your physical spaces to match the balance provided by the earth. If you need to get rid of items, do so in an eco-conscious way. If you need to provide yourself with more, then do that in an eco-conscious way as well. You should start to notice that your physical world doesn't feel like a burden but like it is just enough. You can redo this spell as needed, but be sure to use new dirt each time. The old dirt can go back to the earth.

51: Mars Spell

Mars is the energy of the warrior standing at the edge of the world, ready to conquer. Though most of us will not go into physical battle, we may find ourselves in situations where we have to stand behind our convictions; where we have to be the force for change; where we have to call back down our ancestral lineage and say we are not done fighting. In this case, fighting does not have to equate to violence. There are hundreds of ways to fight for what you believe in without causing harm. When you need the courage to stand behind your convictions, this spell can provide just that bit you need.

What You Will Need
+ Ground black pepper
+ Extra-virgin olive oil

+ A red chime or votive candle
+ A knife or candle carver
+ Charcoal block
+ Lighter or matches
+ Mars planetary incense, such as mustard seed
+ Red dirt in a bowl or a small piece of iron (It is better if the iron is slightly rusted.)
+ A shield, spear, or eagle emblem (This can be anything from a drawing to a piece of jewelry.)
+ An offering of gingerbread and ale
+ *Optional:* athame

Preparation

Make sure the black pepper is finely ground. Drop a few pinches into the oil and stir it. Carve the Mars planetary symbol on your candle.

Then anoint it with your oil and pepper blend. Wash your hands well afterward. Light the charcoal block and let it smolder. Then place the incense on it.

Instructions

Place your candle in the bowl of red dirt. Make sure it is secure enough to not fall over. If you have iron instead of dirt, place it at the base of the candle. Light the candle.

With your hands on either side of the candle so that they encircle it, begin to call to Mars using your voice of power (chapter 4). Say the words slowly and with purpose.

> *Mars.*
> *Mars.*
> *Mars.*
> *Warrior. Commander. Challenger.*
> *Mars.*
> *Mars.*
> *MARS.*

Light the candle, and continue with the words,

> *Champion. Conquerer.*
> *I ask your aid.*
> *Give me the courage to know where I stand.*
> *Give me the mind to know when to fight and when to*
> * resign.*
> *Give me the power, Mars, I ask*
> *To change what I can change and to leave the rest.*

Waft some of the smoke from the burning incense toward you. Let it cover your hands. Let it float to your wrists. Rub it on your neck and your chest.

Now take the emblem and roll it around in the red dirt or touch it to the iron. Then run it through the smoke. And finally, dab some of the oil blend onto it. Hold it up and say,

> *Blessed by Mars,*
> *You are anointed.*
> *Whenever command is needed,*
> *I carry thee.*

Whenever I fight for change,
You empower me.

Set the emblem at the base of the red candle.

If you normally use an athame to bless your cakes and ale, do so now. If not, place two fingers on the plate or cup and say,

I bless this offering to Mars.
May it be accepted.

Repeat these steps for the food and then the drink. Leave them on your altar or in your working space until your candle burns down. Then put on your emblem (or put it aside if you don't want the Mars energy quite yet). Place the food and drink outside. Make sure that you are well-grounded before you leave this ritual space.

52: Jupiter Spell

This spell is designed to increase your circle of influence. Jupiter is the largest planet in our solar system. This means that it has an intense gravitational pull. If you are trying to utilize your pull in a situation to gain success or abundance, this spell can help you. Just be cautious, because too much of anything can quickly become more than you bargained for.

What You Will Need
+ Charcoal disc
+ Lighter or matches
+ Firesafe container
+ Sage, lemon balm, and dandelion, all dried
+ Mortar and pestle

+ The Wheel of Fortune card from any tarot deck,
  or a copy of the image
+ Seafoam green taper or votive candle

Preparation
This spell should be done on a Thursday for maximum efficacy.

Instructions
Light the charcoal disc in the firesafe container. Then grind the herbs together using your mortar and pestle. Put two pinches of the herb mix on the disc and let it smolder.

Take the Wheel of Fortune card from your deck and let the smoke from the herbs waft over it briefly.

Set the card before you. See yourself as the wheel, able to move things, able to move loads no matter how heavy they are. See yourself as the center of the wheel, able to move the things you need from point A to point B, then on to C effortlessly.

Light the candle and call to Jupiter:

> *Jupiter, Jupiter, Chief of the Gods,*
> *Lord of Lightning,*
> *Your influence and power*
> *I call from afar.*
> *Let your influence become mine.*
> *Let me shape, let me make, let me create*
> *The world around me.*

Again, pick up the Wheel of Fortune card. If you are using a Rider-Waite-Smith-based deck, you will likely see that the wheel is like a shield, in that from the center you can reach anywhere else. Focus on the center of this wheel, follow the lines coming out of the center, and look at how they transverse the wheel. If they kept going, they could reach anywhere, any point in time.

See yourself as the wheel, able to move things. Depending on the deck you have, you may see alchemical symbols. Alchemy was an early science that focused on transforming one material into another. This is what you're doing: transforming the world around you into something else, influencing change.

Sit for as long as you need to and let the card speak to you. What else does it say? Are there any mysteries it reveals? Try to visualize what it looks like to have the type of influence you want. What will you do with it? How will you keep from abusing it? What does it look like to be influential in your world?

53: Saturn Spell

It takes Saturn 29.46 earth years to orbit the sun.[8] This makes Saturn a great planet to work with for those long-term goals. You might not get the quick results you would see from a planet like Mars or Venus, but investing time in Saturn is worth the rewards. For this spell, you will be empowering yourself to wait for rewards that could take years to manifest. You will be thinking ahead and preparing for future endeavors.

What You Will Need
+ 8 seeds
+ 4 pots for the seeds, 2 seeds in each pot
+ Soil
+ *Optional*: a mini rake

---

8. "Saturn," Jet Propulsion Laboratory, NASA, accessed January 25, 2024, https://www2.jpl.nasa.gov/solar_system/planets/saturn_index.html.

Preparation

Do this spell on a Saturday when the earth is just beginning to thaw. Ahead of time, think of eight goals that you want to manifest over the next few years to decades.

Instructions

One at a time, pick up each seed and place it in between the palms of your hands. Repeat the word or intention you want to manifest eight times. Bury two seeds in a pot. Using your finger or the mini rake, draw the number "8" on the soil.

Repeat this with each of the seeds. Water the pots and place them in a sunny window. Then tend the seeds. Do not panic if they don't all grow. You have still planted your intention. Alternatively, you can plant the seeds outside when it is warm enough to do so. Just return to the spot from time to time and water the area or pick up trash, something to nurture your seeds. Encourage your plants to grow. If they do, it strengthens the magic.

The next part of this spell is where you start taking steps to manifest your goals. If you want to be a college graduate in ten years, then order a course catalog and flip through it. If you want to travel, order a passport. Make the first step so that other steps can follow.

54: Uranus Spell

The connection that Uranus has to progress and innovation should not be discounted, but it is discovery that will be the focus of this spell. By discovering physical spaces, perhaps even ones not far from you, you are allowing yourself to be open to discovering your interior world as well. When exploring, be sure you do so safely. That cave an hour from your home may be enticing, but if you're not a professional spelunker, pick someplace else. On that note, the place you choose to explore does not have to be any grand affair; it can be a park you've never been to or a new city. As long as it is new to you, it will suffice.

What You Will Need
+ Get your stuff. You're going outside. Put together anything you will need to be safe and comfortable in your exploration.
+ Snacks and water
+ A map app or traditional map
+ A notebook
+ Something to write with

Preparation
None.

Instructions
This spell is about the experience. So while it's tempting to post pictures of your excursion, try to keep your phone in your pocket and let yourself wander the new area. As you do so, look, be present, and really see the area you are exploring. Let your intuition guide you on where to go. Take your time. This is not a race where you have to arrive at the end. It is an opportunity to get to discover your world, your surroundings, and yourself.

As you journey, find a spot (or several) where you can pause for a moment. Eat a snack and drink some water. Use this opportunity to make notes in your journal about images, thoughts, patterns, or anything that strikes you as important. Write about your discoveries. Write about what you have discovered about yourself. If nothing comes to you on that trip, it's okay. Do it again, this time in a new spot. Self-discovery is a process.

55: Neptune Spell

Dream spells are fairly easy to find. What sets this one apart is that you will be receiving messages about empowering your life and yourself. Since Neptune is the Roman god of the sea, and water corresponds to the ability to receive psychic messages, working within this realm can awaken your senses. You may find that after you perform this spell, especially multiple times, you are more receptive to the hidden world than you were before. In this spell, you will be empowered through your dreams.

What You Will Need

+ A purple piece of fabric, roughly 5" square
+ The following dried herbs: chamomile flowers, rose petals, and a sprig of baby's breath (stalk removed)
+ Silver ribbon long enough to tie a bow
+ A silver marker
+ Lavender oil
+ A pen
+ A journal, notepad, or piece of paper

Preparation

Do this spell before bed. Complete the first part, where you make the sachet, before starting your sleep routine. Make sure you have fresh linens on your bed. If there is anything specific you need to do before bed to ensure you will sleep well (such as wearing socks, reading for twenty minutes, putting on your favorite pajamas, etc.) do this as part of your spell. Make it part of the ritual.

Instructions

Take your purple fabric and place it on a flat surface. When you place the chamomile in the center of the cloth, say, "That I may cross safely into the dream world, purified, protected, and empowered."

When you place the rose petals in the center of the cloth, say, "That my dreams will be sweet, though they be revealing."

When you place the baby's breath in the center of the cloth, say, "That I may sleep like a baby, comforted and protected."

Now fold the fabric to make a bundle and tie it together with the silver ribbon. Draw (to the best of your ability) a dolphin using the silver marker. Dolphins have a strong association with the Roman god Neptune and will help you attune to his energy.

When you are done, dab on some lavender oil and say, "A dolphin to guide my journey, safely in and safely out."

Place the sachet under your pillow or inside your pillowcase and go to sleep. Keep the journal and pen next to your bed. When you wake up the next morning, record as much of your dreams as possible. Pay close attention to any symbols or themes that stand out.

56: Pluto Spell

Pluto's status as a dwarf planet does not diminish its magical status. If you want to empower self-transformation and rebirth into a new being, Pluto is the planet (and god) to call on for assistance. Rebirth is one of the most revealing and empowering processes a human being can go through. In this spell, you prepare to undergo the process. Do note, though, that this is not a one-off spell. Each time you perform it, you will go deeper and in a different direction than you did before.

What You Will Need
+ At least 3 large candles for illumination
+ Lighter or matches
+ A black taper candle
+ Cedarwood essential oil
+ A black mirror
+ A snake representation

Preparation
First, light the illumination candles to check and see if they provide enough light. If they do not provide enough light, add three more. You should be able to see what you are doing but still have an ambiance. Add candles until you achieve this effect.

Instructions
Anoint the black candle with cedarwood. Place it above the black mirror and light the wick.

Hold the snake representation in your left hand. Gaze into the reflection of the flame in the mirror.

Now hiss. Let the air leave your mouth slowly. Begin to see yourself reflecting through the mirror; see your face take the shape of a snake. Move your body as a snake would move. Continue to hiss.

With the movements of a snake, transfer the snake representation to your right hand. As you do so, see it taking your old outer skin with it. This skin is composed of all the things you no longer need. As the old skin leaves, it leaves behind a supple, fresh layer. This is the new skin of your rebirth. Once the snake is completely in your right hand, hold its face next to yours, again gazing into the flame reflected in the mirror.

What do you see? Look with a soft eye. If you try to force images, they will not come. If you see only the flame, that is not a cause for concern. We all have different gifts—those that come naturally and those we must work to develop over time.

Chapter 6
The Archetypes of Self

The idea of working with archetypes for better self-awareness has had a rise in popularity, as it should. Throughout this chapter, you will be working with personal archetypes or deep aspects or pieces of you. Where a societal archetype is easily recognizable to a group, such as Santa Claus, a personal archetype will be more nuanced. You may have already heard of the shadow archetype before. This is the hidden and sometimes damaged parts of ourselves, the ones we are ashamed of or want to avoid. It is often repressed, and we may not see it until we start looking. But the shadow is not the only archetype that influences our deepest sense of self. This chapter will look at many of the archetypes, including the shadow, that influence our deep-seated behaviors.

Preparation for the Work

When you face the archetypes, you are looking at harsh realities and reaching a place of acceptance of them. There is no spell to undo the past, but we can move beyond it. As you begin your journey into this work, know that it is not easy. With this in mind, this chapter will start with ways to prepare yourself to do this work. Remember, it is not a race, but something to be undertaken one step at a time with patience and kindness toward yourself.

In the first chapter, you were given ways to create a safe space. Before you proceed with this work, make sure that you have utilized one or more of those methods to give yourself a space that is physically safe to work in. Physically preparing yourself for archetype work should also include eating a meal before you begin, making sure your clothes are clean, having your coffee, and doing all the other things that your body physically needs to sustain itself. This means you should be fed, hydrated, and as fully rested as possible.

Mental preparation tends to be a bit more challenging. You can start by mentally telling yourself "I am ready to undergo shadow work" and "I am prepared for the work ahead." Shadow work, though challenging at times, is not dangerous if you have a support system in place. This can be a closemouthed friend, therapist, spiritual leader, or anybody who you feel will be safe to confide in and receive honest feedback from. It's also a good idea to have an outlet such as journaling, art, exercise, or something similar so you have the ability to step away and recenter yourself.

57: Shadow Work Ritual

I will begin with a working that confronts the shadow side of yourself. Before you perform the following ritual, make sure you are not emotionally keyed up or mentally drained. You want to be in a steady mental space before you attempt this spell. The two candles represent the Greek Hekate and her twin torches. By sitting in between them, you will be ensuring you are in the space of balance that Hekate provides. For the image of the shadow self, you can make one or print one off. While it can be anything you like, remember your shadow self is part of you. Keep that in mind while you pick the image.

What You Will Need

+ A white taper candle
+ A black taper candle
+ Lighter or matches
+ An image representing the shadow self
+ A mirror or other reflective surface

Preparation

Set up the candles so that the white candle is to your right and the black candle is to your left. Place the image of your shadow self in front of you, just below the mirror.

Instructions

Light the candle on your left and say in your voice of power (chapter 4),

> *Hekate, Hekate, Balanced One,*
> *Help me bring darkness into the light of dawn.*

Light the candle on your right and say in your voice of power,

> *Hekate, Hekate, Keeper of Spaces in Between,*
> *Help me bring light to the darkness in me.*

Look at the mirror; now look at the shadow self image you have chosen. The shadow self is not something to be feared, but it does deserve to be acknowledged. Stare at the image and say in your voice of power,

You are me and I acknowledge you.
You are me and I acknowledge you.
You are me and I acknowledge you.

Close your eyes. Now you will enter the meditation part of the ritual (see below).

When you return, hang up the image of your shadow self on your mirror or someplace where you will see it every day. If you feel called to select a new image after the meditation, then do so.

Make yourself a good meal and leave some as a thank-you to Hekate for her guidance.

58: Shadow Work Meditation

This meditation works quite nicely with the previous spell. In it, you will also be reinforcing your mental preparation to do work with all the archetypes of self. As previously stated, this is not easy and gentle work. By preparing yourself, you are signaling that you accept the work and are ready for the challenges that lie ahead.

Begin Meditation

Close your eyes and get into your preferred position to meditate. You stand in an open space. Everything on the right side of your body is bathed in a glowing light. Everything on the left side of your body is in darkness. Walk forward, keeping yourself balanced in that space between light and dark.

You walk along this space until you come to a door that seems to come from nowhere but is attached to everything. Run your hand over the door. How does it feel? Is it familiar? Is it old or new? Slowly you open the door, cautiously but without fear.

You hear an ancient voice tell you to come in. As you walk inside, you notice that now daylight is on your left and darkness is on your right. Hekate holds up a hand and points to your left. You see a swirling pattern on the floor. You step into this spot.

She then points to another swirling spot, this one where your right-hand side was. You step into it.

She then points to a third, this one brighter than the others. You step into it. This time, as you make the final step, the light and dark begin to swirl around you... dancing bands of light and dark. You walk toward Hekate.

At her feet is a pool of water. You look into it, and you see your shadow self staring back at you. The dark swirling bands head toward the pool of water and merge into your shadow self. But you notice that some of the bands of light have also entered.

You look into the pool again. This time you see your light self looking back at you, and the bands of light begin to merge into the pool. Just as before, you notice that some of the dark bands enter as well. Nothing exists on its own. This is a reminder.

You look into the pool a third time. Now you see your reflection. Just as you are... beautiful. A culmination of all things.

When you look up, Hekate is gone. Where she was sitting, she has left a golden symbol. Make a note of what it is. Then look for the door and exit back into the world that led you here. As you step out of the door and close it behind you, you notice that the world is no longer split into dark and light. Instead, the world is bathed in the dewy light of sunset. Walk slowly back until you feel you are where you started. Then slowly bring your consciousness back into the physical world.

59: The Child Archetype Meditation

Your inner child may manifest as wounded or spoiled. Your inner child may scream for love or forgiveness. Your inner child may be healthy and whole. The important thing to understand is that our child-self is not something external that resides in our past. The child archetype lives with us our whole lives. It is with you now, influencing your decisions. Working with the child archetype can be understandably difficult. With this being said, do not be deterred from doing the work. Push yourself, but also be patient with yourself. Get a little uncomfortable, but not so much that you break.

The child archetype is full of potential and inquisitive. But it is also naive and dependent on others to survive. In this meditation, you will be encouraged to let your child-self be whoever they need to be. Leave your adult ideas of what childhood means behind and let them teach you. Begin by choosing a place to meditate. To whatever extent is possible, fill that space with items that remind you of childhood: maybe drawings or your baby blanket. Get creative. Even if you only have one or two pictures, that's okay. It should not be stressful; do the best you can.

Begin Meditation

Close your eyes. It is a warm summer day. School is out. The sun is shining. You see yourself at your favorite childhood park. Feel the breeze and smell the trees. Hear the birds singing their songs, welcoming you to summer.

You walk over to a swing and see a small child there kicking their legs to get height. They have your hair color and your laugh. They look at you and smile as they let their feet grab the gravel and bring themselves to a stop. You recognize this child. They are you. The mini-you reaches out a hand and asks you to come play. The two of you go to your favorite place in the playground. There, you run and jump and sing and dance and enjoy all the merriment of childhood. Spend time here with this child, talking and playing games.

When the sun begins to set, child-you says, "I have to be home before dark." You nod in agreement. You reach down and give child-you a hug. As you pull away, they place a hand over your heart and look up at you. They say a word, just one word. This word is a gift they are bestowing upon you, something they want your adult self to remember. What is the word? Let it slip out through your lips. Let it be spoken out loud so that it may join the vibrational resonance of the universe.

As your child-self returns home, invite yourself to stay on that playground and watch the sun as it sets. When you are ready, begin to return to the physical space you are in. Once you are back, open your eyes.

60: Birthday Party Ritual for the Inner Child

You may have discovered while visiting with your child-self that there was something you always hoped for that you never got. This doesn't have to be something deep or related to trauma, though it can be. Perhaps there was a doll you wished for one year or a video game. In this ritual, you are going to give your younger self a birthday party. Now, maybe you don't have space for that pony you wanted, but you could gift yourself with a horseback ride. Spend some time considering how to appease this aspect of yourself, then continue on. This is a fun ritual to perform with others if you are all on the same page. You can gather friends and take turns singing "Happy Birthday" to one another. This ritual can be done on your own as well. It may feel silly at first, but it will feel amazing later. Besides, silly should be encouraged way more than it is.

What You Will Need

+ A cake, any type you want (It can be a small, personal size.)
+ 7 birthday candles

+ The gift you have chosen
+ A picture of yourself as a child (One where you look happy is best.)
+ *Optional but encouraged:* decorations, music

Preparation
Decorate your home and your cake. Wrap your gift.

Instructions
Put on your music. Dance. Have the party part of your party. Place the picture of child-you someplace in the middle of the action.

Then bring out the cake and candles and sing "Happy Birthday" to your child-self. Blow out the candles. (Don't forget to make a wish!) Open the gift and say some words from the heart about how this is the gift your child-self always wanted and how by using this gift, you and your child-self are going to build a better, deeper bond.

When you enjoy the gift, take the picture of your child-self with you so that you can both enjoy it.

61: The Primal Self Archetype Ritual

There is something about primal spaces that ignites our ancestral memory. Before cities and towns, humans lived in smaller communities or tribes all over the world. These communities worked together for survival, they celebrated together, and they had methods for resolving disputes. By accessing your primal self, you will cast aside, though temporarily, stressors from the modern world and access a time when survival was all that mattered.

This is a great family ritual activity. You can hand each family member an instrument and dance around the fire.

What You Will Need

+ Mud in a bowl or face paint
+ A drum, tambourine, castanet, or other instrument of simple construction
+ Some music with a strong drum beat
+ An image of Danu or another deity that seems appropriate
+ Incense
+ Food and drink for everyone to share
+ *Optional*: a bonfire and buckets of water at hand for fire safety

Preparation

Ahead of time, you may choose to compile your playlist for this ritual. Then look up symbols to paint your face and body with, or you can draw whatever design comes to mind. Either way, paint symbols on the faces and bodies of all the participants. For many reasons, this ritual should be done either outside or someplace with a lot of room to move around. Start the fire, if using one, before you begin the ritual. And be sure to leave electronics outside of the space, even your music and speakers.

Instructions

Start the music and let it play for a bit to fill the space with tribal energy.

Have every family member enter the dance area by walking through the incense smoke, one at a time. Let those who have entered move how the music calls them to.

Once everyone is in, you may notice the energy changing. Let it. This rite works best when you don't try to control what or how it happens.

As you dance, shout the name of the god or goddess into the air. Clap, cheer, do whatever feels right in the moment. Let everyone dance and move as they shout and give thanks and blessings. There will be a time when the ritual will reach a peak and naturally start to wind down. Let everyone get food and drink when they are ready. Then sit, stand, or keep dancing as you feast. This part is about community, your tribal connection, so share stories and laughs and camaraderie. You will know when it is time to douse the fire, offer your food to Danu (or another deity), and head inside.

Try to avoid the urge to get back on electronics until at least the next day. This way your tribal essence can be in charge the rest of the night.

It is not uncommon to have intense and vivid dreams after such an experience. Leave a notepad by your bed to record any dreams that come to you.

62: The Shape-Shifter Archetype Ritual

The idea of shape-shifting has been around for millennia. In Norse culture, there was shape-shifting from the berserkers. In Native American cultures, shamans were known to transform into animals such as foxes and wolves. The Irish goddess Morrigan is a shape-shifter. In essence, while the physical body of a person may not change, they take on characteristics belonging to the animal, plant, or deity. In an archetypal sense, the shape-shifter alludes to the human ability to pull in characteristics from animals, plants, other people, and other archetypes, and use these to empower ourselves.

Let's say you need to learn to laugh when you're frustrated. You could work with hyena energy. If you want to be more selfless, a Labrador has good energy for that. And if you want to see yourself as important and valuable, well, a cat can teach you that (if they have time between naps). Here is a ritual to do this work.

What You Will Need
+ A charcoal block
+ Lighter or matches
+ Firesafe dish
+ Vervain, dried
+ Artemisia (wormwood), dried
+ A mortar and pestle
+ 3 animal, plant, or deity representations (For this ritual, you will get an owl [wisdom], a fox [cunning], and dried bluebells [kindness]. You can substitute these for other animals and plants later, but for now, these three give a good balance.)

Preparation
Light your charcoal disc and place it in the firesafe container since charcoal discs take a few minutes to get going. Grind the vervain and artemisia together with your mortar and pestle. Vervain doesn't always like to grind easily, so you can always pull out the scissors and cut it into smaller pieces to make the grinding easier.

Instructions
Set the bluebells in front of you. On either side, place the fox and owl images. Put a few pinches of the herb blend on the charcoal disc. Get comfortable in a sitting position.

Let one of your hands dance through the incense smoke while the other holds up the image of the owl. See your hand in the incense transforming into feathers and your arm becoming a wing. Say, "wise," but try to say it as an owl would. Feel your voice shift. Put the image down and let your other hand and arm change into wings and feathers. Look down at your feet. See them shape themselves into talons. The transformation continues up your body, ending with your eyes, which are now large and able to see movement the way an owl does.

Let yourself "fly" around your safe space, arms open. Repeat the word "wise" as often as you feel like it. When your flight is over, nestle back in front of the incense smoke. Add some more of the blend and let your body return to you. If you feel like one transformation was enough for a day, you can stop here. If not, pick up the image of the fox and add some more of the incense blend to the charcoal disc.

This time, as you run your hands through the smoke, your fingers become furry toes and your arms become front legs. Say, "cunning," but say it as a fox would. Look down at your feet; they, too, are now soft and furry, with long nails. You sprout a fluffy tail that dances back and forth. The transformation continues up your body, ending with your ears, which are now large and alert, able to hear even the smallest of sounds.

Let yourself run and jump around your space, moving as a fox would. Repeat the word "cunning" as often as you feel you should. Think about *cunning* and what it means. Return to the incense when you are ready. Let yourself curl up with your tail around you. Then transform back into yourself. Decide if you want to end the ritual or continue.

If you continue, add some more incense, then pick up the bluebells. Let your hands waft through the smoke. This time, one hand transforms into a leaf and the other forms the drooping blue flowers that give bluebells their name. Your feet become roots, and your head folds over your flowery stem. You might need to get creative to say "kindness" as a flower would. But try it until it seems right.

Instead of moving around your space, let yourself sway in place as if you are dancing in the wind. Repeat "kindness" as often as you feel like it.

When you are done, sit and return to human form.

You now know what it is to be a shape-shifter. Try this exercise again with different animals, plants, and even stones, gods, and goddesses.

Other shapes to try: Horse (endurance), zebra (camouflage), lion (courage), sloth (patience), sunflower (warmth), rose quartz (love), and evergreen (longevity).

63: The Magician Archetype Meditation

We can't force the world into change through sheer willpower. What we can do is look for synchronicities in the natural flow of the world. Coincidence is frequently mistaken for synchronicity, but they are not the same. The difference is that coincidence would have us thinking that all of these occurrences with apparent connections happen accidentally. Synchronicity points out that they occur as part of a tapestry of life, like a river collecting soot and soil on its way. The magician, therefore, searches for a way to connect to the tapestry of life and take notice of these synchronous events.

Begin Meditation

Get comfortable. Close your eyes. Take nine deep breaths, full of intention. You begin to feel a cold, still air surround you. You feel the space around you encircle you in the protective womb of Mother Earth. The drip of water from a stalactite above lands on your head. You look around your space and see that the cavern you are in is vast. A glowing blue stream runs in front of your feet. You follow it, through one cavern, then into another, and another.

Through nine caverns, you make your way until you notice you are where the river ends, forming a giant pool of water. Roots from a massive ash tree reach down through the ceiling and touch the pool with their tips. There are three women in front of you—the three Fates. You greet them with reverence, knowing that they are the most powerful of all beings, influencers of the lives of humans and gods.

Spread between them is a large tapestry, the biggest you have ever seen. You marvel at the shapes and the colors.

"I seek to become the magician," you say to them. "I seek to understand the synchronicities of life. I seek to understand how all things fit within the macrocosm."

One of them looks at you but says nothing. The pool in front of you grows darker and deeper; you know that they want you to cross it.

As you enter the pool, you feel the water turn so cold it burns through cloth, through skin. It freezes you to your bones, but you keep going. One step. Then another. Each one tougher, but necessary. When you reach the bank, your skin hurts from the cold. You lift yourself out of the water with the remainder of your strength. Your skin instantly warms, restoring blood flow and feeling to your skin and organs.

They still don't speak, these immortal keepers of life and death, but you feel called forward. One of them points to a spot in the tapestry; you look closer. Some of the threads are frayed, knotted, or burned. Some are thicker or thinner than the rest. She taps again on the tapestry. You notice that some of the threads—in fact, most of them—do not follow a linear path. Most flow, much like the river you followed. Many of the threads branch.

Spend time running your fingers over the tapestry, following threads, exploring colors and shapes and patterns. What do you see?

What are you learning? You hear the snap of scissors and turn to look. At the end of the tapestry, a cord has been cut and a new one has been woven into the gap that remains.

There is one final step before you can leave. One of the weavers hands you a thread. With a steady hand, you weave it in a pattern all its own, looping and tucking it between other threads. You hand the thread back, and she casts a wizened smile in your direction. Though no words have been spoken, much has been exchanged.

When it is time to leave, a bridge appears over the lake, now back to its original bright blue. You cross the bridge and follow the stream back out through the caverns from whence you came. Back in the original cavern, you bring yourself back to the sacredness of the space you are sitting in. When you are back in the mundane world, open your eyes and reflect on all the tapestry has taught you.

64: The Addict Archetype Meditation

We live in a society of more, more, more. More money, bigger houses, more cars; it is never enough. When you combine this proclivity with challenging life events, it is no wonder so many struggle with addictions. Most people think of addictions as being alcohol and drugs. While this is accurate, addictions can also exist around codependency, gambling, social media, technology, sugar, validation seeking, adrenaline, and more. In this meditation, you will discover what your addictions are so you can recognize and release them.

Light four candles (tealights are fine) and have them surrounding you while you enter this meditation. The first time through, you will enter the cave furthest to the right. The next time you come, choose a different cavern. The meditation will become more intense each time you do it.

Begin Meditation

Close your eyes and see yourself in a desert. You sink to your ankles in the sand that surrounds you as far as you can see. You take a few steps forward then stop, this time sinking down to your knees. You walk a little farther, this time sinking to your thighs when you stop.

It is very hard to move, but somehow you manage a few more steps before movement becomes impossible. Now you are held in place, but you sink. Though the sand is rising, you are unafraid. You let it take you down. You let it carry you into deeper and deeper levels. Feel the weight of the sand. Let it rest against your body from all sides. Let it help push you, creating more and more pressure.

Finally, your feet feel weightless. They are dangling in the air. You keep dropping slowly, unsure of what, if anything, is beneath you. When your hips and torso are free from the sand, you fall. Luckily, the drop is not far, but you still land with a thud.

You find yourself in a cave. It is dark and dry, illuminated by four oil lamps. You look around and see there are many branches in this cave. How many do you see? Take an oil lamp from off the wall. Pick the opening farthest to the right and enter it.

This cavern shows you some of the things you overuse. What it contains might be things you depend on, abuse, or are addicted to. It is for you to decide which. See them surrounding you. Check in with yourself. How does it make you feel to be surrounded by them? What would it feel like if this space was empty? As you leave, a door appears. Make sure to close it as you walk through it into the next room.

Again you are in a cavern. It contains one of each of the objects from the previous cavern. They are on a platform. When you are ready, walk to the first item. Tell it, "I like you. But I don't need you. With this goodbye, I begin my return to wholeness." Beside the item is a button. If you press the button, that item disappears into the sand below. Are you willing? Do you push it?

One by one, repeat the words and decide what buttons you are willing to push and which you will ignore. When you have circled around, stand in the middle of the small cave. You are naked, vulnerable, but freer than you have felt in months. A stalactite drops from the ceiling; you grab onto it and it pulls you up, returning you to the surface of the sand. Once there, you can make your way back into the realm of consciousness and slowly open your eyes. Throughout the days and weeks and months that follow, pay attention to your interactions with the items you saw in those caverns. Are you more aware of them? Are you more aware of your behavior regarding them? Is there anything from your meditation that you can get rid of or use less in the real world?

65: The Artist Archetype Ritual

Creating art is something humans do instinctively from the time we can hold a crayon. Some of us will keep creating art throughout our lives, but some of us stop nurturing this creative force. We either get led to believe that if we aren't good at it we shouldn't do it (a myth, by the way), or we focus on other priorities. This ritual will help you bring your inner artist out to play so that you can express all the things that can't be said with words alone. This ritual is not about making a masterpiece; it is about expression. No one needs to see this artwork unless you want them to. So don't worry about making something museum quality; make something that is you.

What You Will Need
+ Newspaper or other floor covering
+ Clothes you can get paint, clay, marker, etc. on
+ Music without words (Anything with steady drum beats works well for this.)

+ A mirror you can access
+ Art supplies for your chosen medium
+ A space to work

Preparation
Line your workspace with the newspaper and put on your "art clothes."

Instructions
Turn on the music and look at yourself in the mirror. Repeat, "I create. I make. I shape" over and over until you are ready to create. If you are using a paintbrush, put that first splash of paint on your canvas. If using clay, make the first shape with your finger or tools. Try to create with instinct—that is, if you feel the sky should be orange, let it be orange.

As the music plays, start moving your body. Let the movements of your body and the sound of your space be reflected in the art you are creating. How does it feel to create?

Engage in this activity until you find yourself done, ready for a break, or to another natural point of conclusion. This could be minutes or hours.

Return to the mirror and look at yourself again. Do you feel more creative? Does your artist self feel content?

For the next few days, look at the art you have created. Instead of looking for critiques and criticisms, recall what the very act of creating felt like. If you want to add to it or change it, you can. Each time, just repeat the previous steps to contact the artist archetype.

66: The Pauper Archetype Meditation

This meditation is about confronting the fear of not having enough. Survival is a human instinct. This meditation is going to take you outside of affluence and comfort. Even if you live a lifestyle that you would not consider particularly affluent, this meditation can help you gauge your gratitude and tune in to the real treasures that exist in our world.

It is best to be naked or scantily clad for this meditation if you feel comfortable. If not, it is fine to wear clothes, but accessories such as watches, jewelry, scarves, sunglasses, etc. should be removed.

Begin Meditation

Close your eyes. Imagine yourself in a world that is barren and desolate. The sun shines intensely upon you. Feel its rays scorching your skin. All around you, all you can see is sand in every direction—red sand against a vibrant blue sky. You begin to walk, the hot sand burning your feet. You feel an incredible thirst come over you. It burns your throat, making it impossible to swallow. Your body wants to sweat, but you don't have enough water to do so.

Suddenly, the glint of water catches your eyes. You walk toward it. It is not an easy journey, but an arduous one. When you finally reach the pool, you worry that it may be a mirage. But you reach a hand down into the pool anyway. Clear, cool water comes up into your hand. You drink it in, giving thanks as you do so. Feel its droplets sliding down your throat, rejuvenating your cells. Though you have little at this moment, the gift of water makes you feel rich in ways no jewels or gold ever could. Drink in another mouthful. Then another. Drink until your thirst is satiated.

You continue walking, away from the oasis, back into the red desert. You walk, and the sun is high in the sky. Though you aren't given a direction to go, you know the path you are walking is the right one. Walk and walk until the red sand begins to give way to golden fields and green plant life. Your stomach begins to growl loudly. With it comes pain, the pain of hunger. You walk through this landscape—this fertile, lush world—until you come to a garden. On a plant, you see a rich, red tomato growing on the vine. You pluck it and give a thank-you for the nourishment it is about to give your body. As you bite into the tomato, you feel its juices run along your cheek. As you chew, you become aware of the path this tomato has taken from seed to vine to flower to fruit. It fills your stomach in a way no meal ever has before. You and the tomato are part of the same cycle.

You are tempted to stay in this garden, but the sky is darkening with clouds, and you must be on your way. You head out of the garden, out past the fields, and eventually come across a beach. By now, the winds have started blowing and the rain has begun to fall. It is a stinging rain that soaks you, chilling you to the bone. You look around the world and see an alcove, a cave tucked into the side of the cliff. You make your way toward it. The waves from the sea are swelling and crashing into the shore. Though the path is slick, you trust your footing to take you there.

You reach the cave just in time. As you enter, lightning and thunder take over the sky, and the rain falls like a cascade. Inside, you find everything you need to make a fire. In the Paleolithic era, humans had to collect fire or make it using flint. You pick up a book of matches from next to the firepit and strike one. As you light the fire and feel its warmth filling the space and drying your body, see the shadows it casts on the walls. What stories play out in the flicker of the flames?

On your travels, you have known thirst and quenching of that thirst. You have known hunger and the satiation of that hunger. You have known exposure to the elements and the safety of shelter. You have known the cold and the warmth. You have learned what is important and what is life-giving and life-preserving. You can sit and bask in the warmth of the fire for as long as you would like. When you are ready to return, the rain will stop. You may exit the cave. Begin to bring your body, mind, and spirit back into the mundane world.

67: The Healer Archetype Spell

We all have an inner healer. For some, it is more pronounced, but it is there regardless. The next chapter focuses on healing the self. The healer archetype, though, focuses on healing the world. It seems like a big task. It is. That is why we need as many hands working on it as possible. When you connect to your healer archetype, you will see the ways that healing can happen. You will begin to notice opportunities to promote healing in your world.

What You Will Need

- Extra-virgin olive oil
- 4 ramekins or other small containers
- A mortar and pestle
- The following herbs: rose petals (love), sage (wisdom), calendula (kindness), anise (wholeness)
- 4 unused Band-Aids

Preparation

Put some oil in each ramekin.

Grind each herb one at a time. As you grind each herb, think of the word that connects to it and repeat that word out loud several times. For example, "kindness" while you grind the calendula. Add one herb to each ramekin. Mix with the oil. *Note: It is okay if some of the herb is not crushed to powder. The idea is to mix the essence of the herb with the oil.*

Place a Band-Aid in each of the four areas: over your heart, on your brow, on one of your feet, and just below your ribcage.

Instructions

Peel off the Band-Aid over your heart. As you say the words, dab some oil-and-rose mix onto the area. Say, "For hearts hurt by betrayal, I heal them now with love."

Peel off the Band-Aid on your brow. As you say the words, dab some oil-and-sage mix onto the area. Say, "For minds hurt by ignorance, I heal them now with wisdom."

Peel off the Band-Aid on your foot. As you say the words, dab some oil-and-calendula mix onto each foot. Say, "For bodies hurt with violence, I heal them now with kindness."

Peel off the Band-Aid on your ribcage. As you say the words, dab some oil-and-anise mix onto the area. Say, "For spirits hurt by chaos, I heal them now with wholeness."

Sit in silent meditation for as long as you are able. Think about the meaning of each word: love, wisdom, kindness, and wholeness.

If you are keeping a magical journal, write about your experience.

68: The Destroyer and Creator Archetype Meditation

There is no destruction without creation, and there is no creation without destruction. Humans tend to get attached to the idea of making and shaping while ignoring that some things must be swept away to make room.

Think of something you want to create in your world. What stands in the way? This should be something you have influence over. For example, if you want to create space for more creativity, you may need to destroy fear or procrastination. Think of one thing you want to create in your life. Hold it in your mind as you enter this meditation.

Begin Meditation

See yourself in a cluttered space. Maybe it is cluttered with color or belongings or self-doubt. Whatever clutters this area, focus on it. How does it feel? Does your breathing slow? Speed up? What happens to your pulse?

Pick a spot in this space, just one spot, where you want to manifest your creation. Clear that spot. To do so, you will need to physically remove what is there, with either water or earth or air or fire. You will need to emotionally let go of it. And you will need to spiritually cleanse that space. Start with a small spot. Once it is clear, place what you want to grow in that spot. You will see it is small at first, but it gets bigger. It grows and fills the space you have emptied. But there's a problem: it can only grow that far, no further.

Pick a new area next to the one you cleaned before. Repeat the steps of physical, emotional, and spiritual removal of the old. Again, your new intention grows. Clear a few more spaces in the same way. How big will it grow? That depends on how much space you give it.

When your new goal has filled all the space you have cleared and all the old has been removed, spend some time in reflection. How can you carry this manifestation into the physical world? How can you make space for this new goal? What do you need to clear away to give it room to grow? When you are ready, bring your attention back to the physical world and open your eyes.

69: The Revolutionary Archetype Meditation

For this meditation, you are going to put yourself in the mind of a rebellious figure. This meditation is not to train you to go out and cause mayhem but rather to be able to decide what is right and what is true, regardless of what is popular or common. This archetype will challenge you to consider your very notions of right vs. wrong.

It should be noted that this meditation is a guide and not a factual depiction of events. This is a very intense meditation. It could even be jarring, so only go through it if you are comfortable being uncomfortable.

Begin Meditation

Close your eyes. Make a connection with your breath. Think about the space you are in. The walls begin to transform, becoming straw coated in plaster. The floor beneath your feet is wood and creaks when you step on it. In front of you is a mirror. The glass is foggy, but it is clear enough to see your reflection. At first, you see yourself. Then you become transformed. Suddenly you are wearing armor. Your hair is pulled tightly back. In your hand is a sword, shiny and new. It has never seen warfare. There is a loaf of bread, freshly baked, on the table. It is a feast in these times of starvation. You also see an iron key on the table. Though you don't know what it unlocks, you put it in your pocket.

You step out into the air. The scents of hay and grass and dung linger in the air. You walk to the left, down a cobblestone road. Around you are many people, plainly dressed, carrying baskets and linens. The streets are busy and alive. Sitting on a step outside of a single-room house is a woman, old as time, with foggy eyes. She asks the people passing by if they could spare some coins or some food. As you walk past, she reaches out a hand. You hear voices telling you that the woman is near death and there is no reason to help her. As you look at her thin frame, stretched skin resting over bone, you know they are right. There is a sword in your hand and bread in your pocket. At the thought of it, your stomach rumbles. You don't know how long you will be in this world and if you will have another chance for food. What do you do? What choice do you make?

When your decision is made, you walk on. Next, you come upon two men shackled to a wall. One of them calls to you to come toward him. His hair is matted, and his skin is covered with boils. The other one is not in much better shape. You step closer to the first man; the smell of booze emanates from his skin. "Release us," he says, both a question and a command. You pull the key out of your pocket. You only have one key, one choice. "What crime are you in for?" you ask the men.

The first man answers, "Murder."

The second answers, "Theft."

Which man do you release? The answer may seem simple, but after you release one of the men, you see a wanted poster. The one jailed for murder, murdered his daughter's rapist. The one who stole, stole all the money and possessions from that blind woman you passed. Do you still feel confident in your decision? Had you known, would you have made a different choice? Why or why not?

Key and bread gone, there is one more scenario to face. You continue walking down the street. You see a small group of children. They are tied together, about to be burned at the stake. You could take your sword and save these five children with one slash of the sword. However, if allowed to live, one child, you are unsure which, will cause the death of one hundred others, including several children. You can save all five or none. What choice will you make?

Choices made, you turn back down the street. You pass the shackles, and you pass the old woman. You leave your footsteps as you go. You leave the imprint of your choices. Revolutionary deeds do not need to be large. One of the most revolutionary things we can do in life is to question. As you return to the room where you started, allow yourself to breathe. Allow yourself to be comforted by the fact that these choices were made in the safety of meditation. Slowly start to bring yourself back.

When you return, tend to your self-care. Drink water, eat food, and bathe. When you are ready, reflect on what you learned from this meditation. Did it make you see things differently? Do you feel the need to ask more questions?

Chapter 7
Healing and Emotional Engagement

When I first started to consciously work on healing, I found myself facing emotions—a lot of them. I used to stuff them away and avoid whatever emotions I could. Those pesky feelings I had tried so hard for so long to bury in the back of my brain were surfacing because I had now made a space for them to exist.

As you grow and heal and change, you may find yourself becoming more attentive to and aware of your emotions. Soon you will realize that if you are going to experience emotions like contentment, love, friendship, and happiness, you have to be prepared to experience the loss, regret, fear, and sadness that also fill up the emotional spectrum. We don't get to pick and choose what emotions we feel. It's an all-or-nothing deal. In exchange, though, feeling those emotions facilitates the healing process.

70: Opening the Self Meditation

Many people learn to close themselves off from the world. This defense mechanism often starts in childhood. And while there is certainly nothing wrong with protecting yourself, being closed off can prevent you from experiencing life in a way that is deep and meaningful. This meditation can help you gradually open up and step into your role in the world. For this meditation you will want a small purple flower. Freesias (*Freesia corymbosa*) or cosmos (*Cosmos bipinnatus*) work well for this.

Begin Meditation

Start by taking a few calming breaths. Hold the flower in the open palm of your dominant hand. Look at the flower; study its nuances. What parts of the flower do you find particularly appealing? When you feel you have explored the details of this little flower, close your eyes. Focus on seeing the flower in your mind's eye. When it is fully in focus, breathe in and see the petals closing. As you breathe out, see the petals open. Play with the speed of your breath. Do the petals open and close to match your pace?

Return to your natural breathing speed. This time, as you breathe in, visualize the purple flowery essence entering your body. It may take a few breaths for your body to be filled with the flower essence; keep going until it is. When you feel that the purple energy is flowing throughout you, focus this energy along your spine. You may notice that some areas of your body want to take in more of the energy than others; allow this to happen.

You should now have areas of purple—pockets, if you will— within your body. Focus again on your breath. And just as you saw the petals of the flower open when you exhaled, so too will each of these energy pockets. Attend to each one, making sure to get it to open completely before you move on to the next one. Work your way through them slowly until all are opened.

Once this happens, begin to return your consciousness back to the room you are in. Become aware of the flower in your hand, the ground beneath you, the clothes on your body, and when you feel as though you are back in the physical plane, slowly open your eyes.

71: Feel Emotions Meditation

One of the tricky things about emotions is that we have to be able to feel all of them or we don't get to feel any. Right along with love and passion and being elated are sadness and grief and being forlorn. In this spell, you will give yourself permission to feel any emotions, all emotions. Here's the trick, though: feeling the emotions without letting the emotions consume you. This meditation can be intense, so if you feel the need to try it in parts, that is fine. You can leave anytime you need to.

Create a safe space for yourself. Put an obsidian in your pocket or somewhere you can easily reach it from your meditative position. If at any time the emotions get to be too much, you can squeeze the stone, focus on your breathing, and return to your safe space.

Begin Meditation

You are going to breathe intentionally for several moments. Make your breaths deep and purposeful. When you feel like you are at an emotionally even level, you may close your eyes, and with one more intentional breath, see yourself at the base of a mountain. The mountain is a single peak. It stands high against the bright blue backdrop of sky. It is beautiful around you, the most perfect space. Let this space fill you up with happiness and delight before you look up.

For as you look up, you see the top of the mountain is hidden behind dark clouds.

Begin your ascent up the mountain. As you climb, you notice that your hands are not touching dirt; they are touching volcanic ash and igneous, volcanic rocks. These are black and porous. They were created when the mountain last erupted. You keep climbing, aware of the seething mountain below you.

The wind picks up. It swirls against your skin and makes your footing shaky. You climb on. Halfway up the mountain, you grab a handhold, and it slips and falls, cracking against the stone below you. You look down. The rock seems to fall into eternity. What do you feel? Are you exhilarated? Anxious? Let yourself sit in the feelings, uncomfortable or not. When it is time to climb again, you thank the feelings for their presence, but you know that you must climb on.

You are now at the cloud line. Visibility is low as the clouds fill all the empty space around you. You look up, and projected on the cloudy backdrop are the images of all the family and loved ones who have passed. Some of them may speak to you. Others may not. But listen to their voices, their words, their vibrations. They turn, and they look at all of those they have lost. Then they face you again, countless dead eyes. All at once, they begin to weep. Their tears bring on a rainfall. It coats your skin. You know that this is not the average rain; this is the saline rain of tears—their tears. Their sadness flows over you. What do you feel? Do you join in their sadness? Do you delight in seeing their faces? Do you feel many things? Some identifiable, others lost?

Thank these spirits for letting you feel sadness, but acknowledge that now is the time to move forward. The rain subsides, leaving the stones slick. No matter. You begin your climb again. You reach the peak this time. Look out over the world. You have successfully climbed through happiness and anxiety (or exhilaration) and sadness. But this is only part of the journey.

A rumbling noise catches your attention. You turn to face it just in time to see magma flowing out of the mouth of the volcano. Inside, the magma swirls. It belches and burps slowly at first, but it speeds up. For a moment, your feet feel frozen in place. But then the logical, rational side of you takes over. You begin to move quickly down the mountain. You can feel the heat from the lava right behind you. You look back; it is close enough to threaten to consume you. It gets hotter; you know that it is closing in. With too much of the mountain to go, you know you cannot outrun this. You spot a stone outcropping. Take shelter under it.

The lava is fast now. It flows over the stone and around it, but you are protected in this outcropping. It is hot. It is uncomfortable. But you are safe. It flows and flows, seeming to never let up. Then it eases closer to you. It looks as if it might touch you. You scream. It is such a primal scream that the birds chirp in response and the trees shake and the clouds part. You let that scream out until your lungs are raw. The lava slows as your scream dies down. When it stops, so does the lava. It begins to cool and solidify next to you.

You wait until you know the lava has cooled. Then you take a few deep breaths and finish your descent down the mountain. As you walk, you see that new, green life is sprouting. Where there was turmoil and anger there is now new life developing from its release— new life nourished by your new understanding of emotions.

At the foot of the mountain, you look up and remember all you have seen and done this day. Focus on your breathing and begin returning back to your physical self. Grab the piece of obsidian and let it bring you back into your body. Take as much time as you need to get back. If you keep a meditation (or similar) journal, record the experiences you had.

72: Regulate Your Emotions Spell

We don't get to pick and choose what emotions we feel. If you are unused to feeling emotions—for example, if you grew up in a household where they were not expressed, you have severe childhood trauma, or you spend time drinking or using drugs—they can feel like storms raging out of control.

In this spell, I have given you just two emotions to start with: sadness and happiness. You will find a flower that represents each of these emotions. I have suggested a flower for each below, but you can pick other flowers or substitute stones or colored strips of paper. You can also opt to work on a different set of emotions.

What You Will Need
+ A blue candle
+ A yellow candle
+ Lighter or matches
+ Blue lily (*Agapanthus praecox*) for sadness
+ Yellow daylily (*Hemerocallis lilioasphodelus*) for happiness

Preparation
Set up your sacred space. Light the candles.

Instructions
One at a time, run the flowers over the flame of their corresponding colored candle. Be sure to keep them at a safe distance. Now pick up the blue lily. Smell it. With purpose and intention, hold it up to your nose and let the scent overwhelm you. Let it coax you toward a sad thought or memory. Now close your eyes. See yourself standing in front of a giant blue lily. It is big enough that the petals could envelop you.

The flower bends down, and a petal lifts for you to step inside. The petals close around you. Within the petals, you are consumed by sadness. You feel it in your bones and in your skin. Focus on that memory that was originally brought up when you smelled the flower. Let yourself go there. I know it is uncomfortable, but you don't have to stay there long. Once you feel like you are consumed by sadness, you will begin to peel open the layers of petals that surround you.

The first petal allows in some fresh air, fresh perspective. Next, you open the petal across from that. This petal brings in time, which is the ultimate healer. Repeat this for each of the six petals. Three brings in understanding, four brings stability, five brings hope, and with the sixth, you are released.

Now pick up the yellow daylily. Just as you did with the blue lily, you will smell it and let it coax a happy memory forward. Once again, you will close your eyes and see yourself in front of a giant yellow daylily. It surrounds you with its petals, just as happened before. Let yourself be carried into the memory. Let the happiness fill up your body, every cell, and your very skin. You enjoy your time here but notice that the happiness begins to feel surface level after some time. It may even bring on a state of frenzy. As you peel the first petal, you become aware that there are many degrees of feeling between happiness and sadness. The second petal brings you time. Three brings understanding, four brings stability, five brings hope, and with six, you are released.

You may notice that the petals in the second flower bring in many of the same qualities you got with the first. That is, at least in part, because there is much overlap between emotions. You can feel sad and elated at the same time. You can care about someone you are mad at. Emotions seldom exist on their own. When you have practiced this spell, you can bring in some of the emotional complexities to give yourself an extra challenge.

For now, return to your space. Let the candles burn, and place the flowers outside to let them be returned to the earth.

73: Heal Your Inner Child Spell

Not everyone has significant trauma in their childhood. If you don't, that is fantastic. You can still use this spell as a way to strengthen your inner child. If you do have trauma, this spell can be used in addition to counseling to help the healing process.

What You Will Need
+ A picture of yourself as a child
+ A few trinkets that remind you of things that made you happy as a kid (Examples: A picture of a dog, a skateboard keychain, etc.)
+ A doll, figurine, action figure, or stuffed animal to represent your childhood self (It doesn't need to look like you; it is a symbolic stand-in.)
+ Some Band-Aids, bandages, and cotton balls
+ 1 white taper candle
+ Lighter or matches
+ Peppermint or lemon essential oil

Preparation
Attach the picture of yourself to the item you're using as a stand-in. You can use tape, a safety pin, a paperclip, or string. If you don't want the photo damaged, make a photocopy and use the copy. Surround the stuffed animal or doll with all of the reminders of your childhood.

Anoint the candle ahead of time and place it a safe distance away from the stuffed animal or doll.

Instructions

First, close your eyes and take some deep breaths. Think back to a moment of genuine childhood happiness. It could be getting a bike, opening presents, hugging your mom—any memory at all, as long as it's happy. If this is difficult for you, imagine what one of these moments could have—should have—felt like. Let that feeling fill you up. Hold onto that feeling the best you can while you open your eyes.

Place your hand over your heart. Light the candle, and as you do, say, "May this candle light my way to healing."

Dab some of the essential oil on your chest where your heart rests and say, "May my heart be full of love."

Dab some oil on your brow and say, "May my mind be full of wisdom."

Dab some oil on the back of each hand and say, "May my hands be full of compassion."

You are going to now repeat the process, but this time on the stand-in.

On its chest, say, "May your heart be full of love."

On its head, say, "May your mind be full of wisdom."

On its hands, say, "May your hands be full of compassion."

Finish by holding up the stand-in and saying, "I am you and you are child me. It's my will. So shall it be."

Give child-you a hug. Hold the hug as long as you want to, as long as you need to. Feel this hug going to your child-self. Feel this hug embracing you in the past at all the times you needed it.

Set the child-you at eye level, or as close as you can. This next part should be done one step at a time, slowly, and with intention.

Look at child-you and say, "I love you."

Let the words fill the space. Repeat them if it feels appropriate to do so. Feel these words resonating within you and your child-self. Repeat the steps with some of the following phrases:

+ "You are worthy."
+ "I'm proud of you."
+ "You are enough."

Let yourself express any emotions that come forward during this process. You may have tears, laughter, the urge to sing, or another expression. Whatever wants to happen, let it.

You should add any positive and affirmative phrases you feel are necessary or helpful. The important part is to make sure that the words are spoken with thought and intent.

When you have said all you need to say, end with another hug and say, "I love you, child me. I love you, adult me. I love you, future me. So it shall always be."

74: Letter to Let Go Spell

We don't forgive other people for their sake; we do it for ours. Holding onto anger, resentment, and pain is like sipping on poison every day. Yes, we are allowed to have anger and hurt feelings, but at some point, it is beneficial to move past them and remove their power over us. This spell will help you do just that when you are ready, and not before.

What You Will Need
+ Pen with blue ink
+ A piece of parchment paper
+ Blue candle
+ Lighter or matches
+ Fireproof vessel to burn the paper

Preparation
For this spell, you will be writing the letter while you are in the ritual. But if you want to have a rough draft available before you begin, you can do that and copy it over.

Instructions
Write a letter on the parchment in blue ink. It will be addressed to the person you are angry at. It should have a repeated idea or cadence, such as:

> *To [So-and-So],*
> *For that time you [what they did], I forgive you.*
> *For saying [what they said], I forgive you.*

List out all the things you feel comfortable listing. The very last line should read as follows: "For holding onto this anger, I forgive myself."

Then sign it.

Light the blue candle and spend a moment or two calming your mind. By candlelight, read from the letter out loud. When you have read through it, light it on fire using the candle flame and let it burn in the bowl.

The next day, scatter the ashes to the wind.

75: Bad Day Spell

We all have bad days. They come out of nowhere. We just wake up and the car won't start, we spill coffee on ourselves, we get stuck in traffic, and our boss yells at us. Before we know it, we are nearly in tears. The good news is that any bad day can be restarted. Perhaps that sounds like something you'd see on a motivational poster, but it's true nonetheless.

What You Will Need
- Running water
- *Optional:* lavender essential oil

Preparation
None.

Instructions
Stop. When you find yourself about to be worked up in a bad-day frenzy, stop everything. That email can wait, I promise. Go to the nearest bathroom or sink. Turn on the cold water and put your hands underneath it. Let the water run over them.

If you feel the need to cry while the water of emotion runs over your skin, then cry. Cry out all the sadness and anger. When you've got all the cries out, dry your eyes. Stand up tall and breathe. Breathe in and out slowly for a count of five. Repeat five times.

The last step will be to evoke the god or goddess that has a connection to the day of the week you are on. If it's Sunday, call on Sunna, Sol, or Helios. On Monday, call on Selene. Tuesday is Tyr. Wednesday is Woden/Odin or Hermes. Thursday belongs to Thor. On Friday, call to Freyja or Aphrodite. And Saturday is for Saturn.

If you have lavender oil, anoint your wrist and say,

> *[Deity name], I give you this day.*
> *[Deity name], I give you this day.*
> *[Deity name], I give you this day.*

Repeat it until you feel the sense that the reset button has been pushed. Then compose yourself and return to your day.

76: Eye of the Storm Meditation

This world we live in is loud, shouty, chaotic, and angry. Now, chaos and anger have a time and a place. But it is easy to get lost in the depths of their bitter embrace, especially when it surrounds you on social media and the news, and when it is all anyone wants to talk about.

Whenever you feel the sickly ick of societal anger impacting your own emotions, or when you feel the world is chaotic around you, use this meditation to calm yourself and bring yourself back to center.

Begin Meditation

Get to a place where you will not be disturbed for a few minutes. Breathe. It all comes back to breath. Close your eyes and focus on the chaos; see it swirling around you like a hurricane. Feel the wind. See the damaged bits flying through the air. The sky above you is dark and thick. Perhaps the words causing everyone to be in such a stir are floating around in the wind funnel. It whips your hair and threatens to whisk you away.

But you are stronger than this chaos around you. You are level-headed against the ire of humanity. You look up and see that you are in the eye of the storm. You are the calm center. While you can't change the chaos, you, standing in the eye, get proof that you don't have to be swept up in it. The chaos teases you, licks at you, and beckons to you. You can feel it but do not give in.

While still looking up, become aware of a clear cone coming down into the eye and surrounding you. It wraps around you, and suddenly, the winds inside this cone cease to blow. The sky above you is blue and peaceful. The earth beneath you is firm. You look out through your protective layer. You can see that the storm rages on. But inside this cone, you are protected—a visitor to the chaos, an observerable to logically assess the situation.

When you feel calm, you can return to the mundane world knowing that your cone is with you. It surrounds you. It allows you to be aware of the world without getting blown away by it.

77: Calm Your Ass Down Spell

We all get angry; it is a human characteristic. We can't just be okay all the time. This is an unfair and unrealistic expectation. However, there are appropriate ways to deal with anger, and there are inappropriate ways. When you find yourself in such a rage that it could be detrimental, use this spell to calm yourself. It is handy because it doesn't require a lot of equipment, and it can be done virtually anywhere.

What You Will Need
+ A length of rope, string, or yarn at least 18"

Preparation
None.

Instructions
You are going to tie and untie knots in this spell. It is designed to use up to five knots (to correspond to the five letters in A-N-G-E-R), but you can use less if needed. Take out your length of rope. As you tie the knots, be as forceful—or not (See what I did there?)—as you need to be.

Tie the first knot and say, "'Ahhhh' is what I want to scream."
Tie the second knot and say, "Now is not the time."
Tie knot three and say, "Gain control of body, mind, and soul."
Tie knot four and say, "Emotions don't own me."

Tie the fifth and final knot and say, "Release, release. Release my anger from me."

By now you should be calm. If you are not, you can release the knots, starting with five. Repeat each phrase you said when you tied them.

78: Understanding Death Ritual

I was told once that death is only hard for the living, as the dead are already in their process. This ritual is not for the person who died. This is a ritual for you. In this ritual, you will be journeying to meet Hel, the Scandinavian goddess who oversees the land of the dead (no relation to the Christian hell). You will have the opportunity to ask her questions about the nature of death.

Hel, for those of you unfamiliar, is one of Loki's children. She is described as having half of her body as vibrant and living, and the other half the blue of a corpse. Her appearance and matter-of-fact nature can be alarming. But she should be more respected than feared.

What You Will Need
+ 1 light blue taper candle, like cold flesh (Black can be used as an alternative.)
+ 1 flesh-colored taper candle
+ Lighter or matches
+ An offering of apple slices and honey, with some set aside for your return
+ An offering of mead or wine, with some set aside for your return

Preparation

For maximum potency, this ritual should be performed on the new moon. Think about the questions you want to ask Hel before you perform this ritual. She is wise and powerful. It is good to be prepared.

Instructions

Take a bit of honey and dab it on each candle. You don't need a lot, just a drop. Light both candles; then, while gazing through the flame, let your thoughts drift and get hazy. Speak the following words, letting your eyes get heavier and heavier as you do so, until they eventually close. Repeat the following text nine times:

> *Hel, goddess, keeper of death.*
> *I welcome you here, from the earthen depths.*
> *The end of life I seek to understand.*
> *What lies beyond in your land?*
> *With apple and wine, I call you.*
> *Nine times I call you.*
> *Nine times I say your name.*

See yourself traveling through the earth below you. Feel the world around you get cold as you travel deeper and deeper. You travel down and see the roots of a giant tree guiding you where to go. Follow the roots until you stand in front of a large gate surrounded by cold, blue flames. You understand that you cannot travel past these gates—not yet, not now.

You wait graciously for Hel. When she comes to you, look upon her face without fear. Welcome her as a friend. Invite her to sit and join you. Let her eat and drink before she speaks. When it feels appropriate to do so, ask her one of your questions. Wait for her response. It may come quickly, or she may think about it. Be patient.

Continue the conversation until the time comes for it to end. Bid adieu to the goddess and thank her for joining you.

Follow the roots slowly back to the land of the living. When you return from your meditation, eat and drink the portion of the offering that you had set aside. Leave the rest outside as a thank-you to Hel.

79: Rain Bottle of Emotions Spell

Emotions are not a bad thing. Even the unpleasant ones are necessary. However, when it comes to spellwork, we don't want to be in a hysterical state. This spell will allow you to "store up" emotional energy and use it in your spellwork without having to affect your own mental state. Storms are a powerful source. In this spell, you will once again use the elements.

There are different energies to rainstorms. Think about the difference between a soft, slow rain and a sharp, stinging one. This spell will take place over several periods of time.

What You Will Need
+ Several watertight jars with lids
+ A pen and a notebook
+ Jar labels
+ A Sharpie
+ A towel
+ An umbrella or a change of clothes

Preparation
You might have guessed from the name of this spell that you need to wait until it is raining. Since you will be standing outside, make sure you are equipped with whatever you need to be comfortable.

Instructions

Take one of your jars and set it outside to catch the rain. Close your eyes and let the rain fall on you. Try to clear your mind. What emotion is this rain? Does it calm you? Do you feel fearful? Content? Energized? Stand in the rain and try to pinpoint one or two emotions that this rain resembles. To help you out, a torrential storm may contain the more virulent emotions and a summer sprinkle could be cleansing. These are just a few examples. The specifics are left to you to discover.

Once you're done, take yourself inside and dry off. Leave the jar in the storm until the storm ends or the jar is full. Then bring the jar inside and put the lid on. Dry off the jar and label it "Rainwater of [emotion(s)]."

Next time you need to utilize that emotion in a spell, pull out the jar and sprinkle some on a candle you are using, or use it with a black bowl for divination. There are many ways you can utilize the water in spellwork.

Repeat the spell with different types of rain and record your results.

80: No Rain Bottle of Emotions Spell

You may live in a place that sees almost no rainfall. Well, fear not. You can use the previous spell with wind, snow, or sand.

What You Will Need
+ Several jars with lids
+ A pen and a notebook
+ Jar labels
+ A Sharpie

Preparation

Since you will be standing outside (if possible), make sure you are equipped with whatever you need to be comfortable. Just like with the previous version, you will need to wait until it is windy or snowing. If you are using sand, such as in a sandstorm, do not stand in the storm. Instead, leave your jar someplace secure and retrieve it once the storm has passed. The same goes for any dangerous weather. If it is not safe to be outside, watch it from your window and perform the actions to the best of your abilities.

Instructions

Take one of your jars and set it outside to catch the elements. Close your eyes. The weather surrounds you. Clear your mind. What emotions does this element bring out? Is the snow a sad snow? Is it comforting? Do you feel upheaval in this storm? Calm? Fear? Try to pinpoint one or two emotions that this storm brings out. A snow that has fat and fluffy flakes will feel different than a blizzard.

Once you feel like you have experienced the emotion of the weather, and long before you suffer wind burns or frostbite, take yourself inside. Warm yourself up, brush off sand, comb your hair—do all the things you need to do to right yourself. Leave the jar in the storm until the storm ends or the bottle is full. Then bring the bottle inside and put the lid on. Dry off the jar and label it "[Snow/wind/sand] of [emotion(s)]."

Next time you need to utilize that emotion in a spell, pull out the jar and sprinkle some on a candle you are using, or use it with a black bowl for divination. If you gathered wind, you can wait until you are in ritual and open the bottle at an opportune time. There are many ways you can utilize elements in spellwork.

Repeat the spell with different types of weather and record your results.

81: Be Present Meditation

This meditation should be done for a minimum of twenty minutes each week. It can be employed when you go for a walk or to an event. It is a conscious meditation, meaning you don't need to close your eyes. For this reason, you can do it anywhere. For this meditation, you will put your phone away. Turn off the TV. Pause your music. Remove all distractions. This meditation is to teach you to be where your feet are.

Go someplace you have been to before. An outside space works best, but an indoor space can also work. Take off your shoes if it is safe to do so.

Begin Meditation

Focus on your breath and let your mind clear. If anything pops into your mind, acknowledge it and dismiss it.

Feel the ground beneath you. Bring the full force of your focus to it. Feel the tension between your body and the solidness of the space. Let yourself feel the texture, the temperature, and the gradation of it. If you are outside, bring your attention to the moistness of the grass or dirt or sand. Now look down at your feet. Visualize color sweeping over the ground beneath you. Then breathe in the scent of it.

Hold your hand with your palm facing down to the earth and say, "I am here."

Bend down and place your palms on the earth. Say, "This space is now."

Let all of the textures and temperature received through your feet come in through your palms and say, "I am in the now."

Repeat the word "now" several times until you understand its meaning.

"No past, no future, only present. I am now."

Slowly stand. As you do, intentionally pull up the energy of the earth with you as you rise. Move your feet, one at a time. Repeat, "I am now."

Then resume your day, ever mindful of your place in the here and now.

82: Letting Go Meditation

Control is an illusion. The more we try to control this world, the more opportunities we miss out on. Think about if you are holding onto a penny. You hold it so tightly, afraid to let it go. But then, a dollar comes along. You can't pick it up because you won't let go of the penny. Sometimes we need to surrender control to let the gods and goddesses guide us. You will miss out on so many moments and opportunities if you are unable or unwilling to let go. This meditation will help you do that.

Sit in a pre-chosen safe space. If you are inside, you may want to choose some ambient nature sounds to meditate with. Wind works well with this meditation.

Begin Meditation

Close your eyes and see yourself in a great, wide-open prairie. As you look down, you see yourself on the back of a horse. You can smell its sweat carried on the wind. Next to you is a saddle bag with a piece of parchment sticking out of the top. You grab it and open it up to reveal the map inside. You recognize one of the landmarks. You can see it in the distance.

Beneath you, your horse lets out a grunt, signaling that it is time to go. Reins in your hand, you give a click to motion your steed on. As you head toward the monument, you become aware of the crunch of the ground beneath your horse's hooves. You become aware of the thick heat of the air around you. Off to your right, a forest comes into view. Your horse begins to turn away from the monument and toward the wooded area. You tug the reins and tell your horse, "This is not the direction of the map." But the horse keeps moving toward the woods.

You try a few more times to get your horse to change direction, but to no avail. As you approach the dark woods, you must set down the reins and let yourself be guided. The woods look ancient. Trees bend and twist in all manner of shapes and directions. The light from the sun vanishes, hidden by the canopy of branches above you. With little light, you must trust even more that your horse knows the way.

You travel for several minutes until you come to a clearing with a stream of sunlight coming in as a beam. There you see an old woman standing next to a cauldron, her back to you. She tells you to get off the horse without turning around. You do as she instructs and walk up to the cauldron.

The liquid within it swirls around and around. A leaf from a nearby tree drops in. Then another. More and more leaves fall, swirling red, gold, green, and yellow. The old woman continues to stir the cauldron. Finally, she turns her face to meet yours. A leaf falls; she plucks it from the air and looks at you. Without a word, she crushes it to powder in her hand. Another falls. Again she catches it and crushes it. You ask her to stop. But she repeats the action one, two, and three more times. Each time, she adds the powdered leaves to the cauldron.

She hands some of the leaves to you; she wants you to crush them. As you do, you notice that your leaves won't crush. They won't bend. They stay as they are. You try harder, for surely if the old woman can crush the leaves, they should be no trouble for you. Try as you might, they won't crush.

The old woman smiles. She closes your cupped hands over the leaves. The leaves begin to move and fall apart on their own. You have created a space to allow change to happen. She signals that she wants you to add your crushed leaves to the cauldron. You do so and watch as they swirl into the leafy, watery mix.

Look into the cauldron. Let the images illuminate your intuition and imagination. A shape forms. What is it? What is it you see? This shape, this image, will help you learn to let go. It will help you release and relinquish your control to make space for new and better things.

The woman scoops up some of the water and puts it in a bottle for you. She wants you to drink. You do so willingly. The symbol you have seen imbues itself within you. It becomes part of you, part of your energetic self. You see yourself reflected in the cauldron…glowing and vibrating with autumn-colored light.

The woman leads you to the entrance of the clearing. There, your horse is waiting. The woman takes the map out of the bag; you see that the destination on the map has now changed to show where you are as the destination. You climb on your horse's back and let him guide you out of the woods and back into the prairie. As you dismount, you rub his nose and give thanks. You look up and see that the woman from the clearing is now steadfastly seated upon the horse's back. You exchange nods with her, and she rides back into the direction of the woods.

As you return to the physical plane, you recognize that you have gained a great deal by letting go. Slowly return to the physical world.

Allow yourself to eat and hydrate. Allow yourself a period of time to rest and reflect. Then for the next few days, weeks, months, and years, permit yourself to relinquish control when opportunities arise.

83: Rigorous Honesty with Self Meditation

Here is another working from Pagan priestess JoyBelle Phelan. This spell concerns healing and truth. Rigorous honesty is most valuable when you apply it to yourself in order to know who you are and understand the value of being honest about your actions. Living in honesty means making the decision to tell the truth, but it also means fully understanding the truth. There is a difference between brutal honesty and rigorous honesty: brutal honesty may come across as harsh, critical, or hurtful and can damage relationships and trust. Rigorous honesty is a practice of being truthful with oneself in a thoughtful, respectful, and empathetic way.

For this meditation, you will need a crystal to provide a focus point. Muscovite for its ability to provide insight and onyx for discipline are useful stones, as are smoky quartz, amazonite, lapis lazuli, charoite, and citrine.

Begin Meditation

Ground and center. Focus on your breath. Feel the minutiae fall away as you connect with yourself. Starting on the first day of the week, think back to your actions. Consider your values. Have you lived according to them today? This week? Since the last time you considered them? There is no need for judgment or self-recrimination here; just observe where you have excelled and where you have fallen short. Be accountable for your actions and their consequences. Avoid blaming others or making excuses. Acknowledge your mistakes, learn from them, and make amends when necessary.

Have you practiced self-care? Be clear about your limits and boundaries, and communicate them to others respectfully. This includes saying no when necessary, taking breaks when needed, and protecting your well-being.

You are simply taking inventory of what you need to work on. Charge whatever crystal or object you have chosen to serve as a reminder of what you need to work on. You can carry this object or leave it on an altar as a reminder. When you feel like you have completed the inventory, forgive yourself for the lapses and celebrate the successes. Be kind to yourself and remember to be kind to others; we are all doing the best we can with what we have.

84: Rigorous Honesty with Self Spell

This next spell was also written by my friend JoyBelle Phelan. It is designed to work with the previous meditation. Just as mentioned before, rigorous honesty starts with the self. Avoid the urge to judge your actions; work instead on accepting the truth of them.

What You Will Need
+ A white taper candle for clarity
+ Lighter or matches
+ The crystal you used in the previous meditation

Preparation
Create sacred space, and ground and center. Cleanse your space.

Instructions
Invoke any ancestors or deities you regularly work with. Light the candle, and hold the crystal in your hand of power. Imagine the flame getting larger, filling the space, casting out any shadows. Chant the

following: "Truth that I seek, come to me. Rigorous honesty clear to see. Thoughts I've hidden are revealed to me. Wrapped in trueness I strive to be."

Repeat this as you hold the stone in your hand as a reminder of your vow to yourself. When you feel that the stone is charged, thank your spiritual guests, extinguish the candle, and close your circle. Carry the stone as a touchstone.

85: Emotional Intelligence Meditation

Emotional intelligence is often talked about, but it may be a new term for you. *Emotional intelligence* or *quotient* (EQ) is a term used to describe how well you understand and handle your emotions. If you have a high EQ, you are more likely to understand the emotions of others you interact with.

The following meditation, another shared by Priestess Phelan, can be used when you are processing something that has occurred with someone around you and you need to create space and understanding.

Begin Meditation

Use the four-fold breath to relax and still your mind: breathe in for a count of four, hold for a count of four, exhale for a count of four, and hold for a count of four. Continue this cycle.

Think about the scenario that occurred; focus on not reliving, but viewing this from a neutral observer's point of view. Imagine walking through, one step at a time, whatever the day held or the interaction with the other party. If you can, imagine with all the senses, creating a full scene. Show, don't tell, if you can.

Offer responsibility for any harsh words you spoke, any eye rolls, or other ways you weren't fully present at the moment. Notice if you feel your pulse starting to race or any other physical sensation that indicates you are reliving that moment. Take a deep breath. Allow it to pass. You are simply an observer here. You are noticing what occurred. It cannot touch you now. You are in a space of learning and understanding to take into the future.

Observe the actions of the other(s). Do not slide into blame or judgment. You are simply noticing and observing. This grants you the freedom to recognize their trigger and emotional responses. This can provide you with the context to understand why they responded in the way they did. It provides you with a perspective that you didn't have at the moment.

Focus on your breathing. Keep it calm, steady, and whole. Fill your diaphragm. Imagine a clear light encompassing the scenario. If clear distracts you, imagine whatever color fills you with calm and ease.

Notice what you can about the situation and become aware of what you need to learn from the emotions. Absorb the lesson to be more prepared next time. Breathe. All will be well.

When you feel like you have learned what you can, honor yourself and the other person. Recognize that we are all doing the best we can. Offer grace.

Close your meditation time however you usually do, ground, and remember what you need to.

Chapter 8
Magic for the Day-to-Day

Peoplefrequently ask me how I manage to separate my day-to-day life and my spiritual one. The answer is simple: I don't. I am as much a Pagan when I eat breakfast as when I cast circle. There is no separation. My witch hat, as it were, never comes off. This chapter is about integration—integrating the seemingly mundane tasks of life into the continuum of being Pagan. Not all magic is big pageantry, smoke, and robes. Magic can happen in the smallest of tasks, such as saving the life of a bee or while riding public transport.

Magic flows through us like blood, like water. In a perfect world, we would always live in a way that aligned with our highest spiritual selves in a place that nurtured our spirit. But we don't live in a perfect world, so just do the best you can. As you perform the exercises in this chapter, you will begin to see how you can find the magical energies all around you and how these energies can coalesce into one magical you.

86: Find Your Calling Meditation

You have probably heard of a "calling" before. What you may not know is that it can change over a lifetime. Though we are led to believe that people should find that "one career" that they can stick with forever, this is an antiquated take on jobs. There is no reason why you shouldn't have multiple callings throughout a lifetime. We change; we grow. Don't be discouraged if you do something for several years and then get called on to something else. It just means you have completed the work you were meant to do, and now it is time to move on.

For this meditation, you will need to gather five items that represent you. These can be anything from an article you wrote in sixth grade to a picture of your favorite animal, a tiara (one of my five), an article of clothing that makes you feel like you, a camera, an instrument, a book you love... you get the idea. The only recommendations are that they should represent the best of you and should be small enough to be placed around you in a circle.

Begin Meditation

Get into your safe space and take a few deep breaths in and out. Put your items in a pile in front of you. One by one, lift each item and gaze softly at it. Ask yourself, How does this fit in with the puzzle of me? When you feel like you understand why that item represents you and how it fits, then place it next to you so that when all items are placed they will form a circle.

Once you have reviewed all of the items, close your eyes, place your hand above each of them, and try to feel what color or vibration that item is putting off. Each one of these vibrations will fill up a section, much like a pie chart, but join in the middle, just above your head.

Ask, either to yourself or out loud, What is my calling? What would the gods and goddesses have me do with my life? What is my path? My purpose? My direction? Visualize all of these energies starting to swirl. They form a spinning cord that connects above your head and makes its way into the expanse of space.

As this cord expands, there will be tiny tendrils, much like a web, that reach out and search for the answers you seek. Let yourself journey and be open to the answers. It is tempting to second-guess the answers, especially if you are not used to receiving guidance in this way, but try to avoid this temptation. The answers you asked for have just been given.

When you are ready to return, visualize all those weblike cords coming back into you and back into the original items. Sit with your eyes closed for as long as you need. Focus on the floor beneath you. Place your hands on one of the objects you brought in. Be present in the physical room. Then, when you are back, open your eyes.

87: Dedication to Your Calling Ritual

When you discover what your calling is, you may want to do a dedication ritual and ask the guidance of a deity, spirit, or entity to help you. The transition into this role may be something that takes place over time or is more immediate. You may also find that as time passes, your calling changes. Acknowledge these things. Life is full of ebb and flow.

What You Will Need
- Lemongrass essential oil
- A dark blue taper candle
- Lighter or matches
- An item or photo that represents your spiritual calling

Preparation

Before you begin, do some research on what deity or entity you want to have aid you. For example, if your calling is to dance or do something related to dancing, you might call on the Greek Muse Terpsichore. If you have been called to protect an area of land, then you could call on the land spirits (*landvættir* in Norse tradition), the Roman Silvanus (protector of forests), or the Greek earth goddess Gaia, just to name a few.

Instructions

Create your sacred space as you normally would. Stand tall before your altar or working space. You should enter into this new purpose with strength and dignity.

Anoint yourself with oil and speak into existence, "My life, my path, what I am meant to be, and who I am. Here in fruition. I create, I dedicate the next phase of my life to fulfilling my calling."

Light a candle and call to the entity you are working with: "No path is walked alone. Spirits, gods, and entities abound. [Entity name], guide me, enlighten me, and show me what steps to take."

Stand or sit gazing (not staring) into the dancing candle flame with the photo at the candle's base. Spend the next few moments considering how this calling could impact your life. What steps can you take to start progressing down this path? What fears do you have? What parts excite you? Take time to ask all the questions you have, even if you don't get answers. When you come to a point of peace about the decision, stand in front of the candle flame, arms outstretched, and say your dedication, something like, "I, [your name], stand here before time and space and in the presence of [entity name] ready to take on the role that I have been given. I shall do my best to fulfill this purpose until the time comes when my path changes or I am no longer the best fit for this duty. I shall honor this calling as sacred."

Now take the oil and dab some onto your thumb. Press the oil onto your left wrist and hold it there for a moment. When you release your thumb, your dedication is complete.

88: Parting of the Ways Ritual

If you are someone who finds you have more than one calling or spiritual job in your lifetime, you can use this ritual to say goodbye to your previous task and move on to the next. With this ritual, you will gracefully acknowledge your previous path and prepare for your shift. The keys to this ritual include honoring the lessons you have learned, leaving the old path without ill feelings, lighting a candle for your spot to be filled, mentally and physically pulling away, and stepping into your new role.

What You Will Need

+ A white seven-day glass candle
+ An item or photo that represents your previous calling
+ An item or photo that represents your new calling
+ An athame
+ Lighter or matches

Preparation

Start this ritual on the new moon.

Set up the candle so it is nearest to the photo that represents your previous calling. The photo or item representing your new calling should be opposite the first photo. For example, if you have your photo of the past calling on the west wall, put the other photo on the east wall. The idea is to have enough space that you can move your seven-day glass candle between the two for seven days. I recommend not having the candle directly on your floor during this process. Instead, it is okay to move it across a mantle or a stone countertop.

Instructions
Create your ritual space, then light the seven-day glass candle.

Stand in front of the object that signifies your past calling. Spend a few moments meditating on what you have learned from it, how you have grown, and all the fond memories it has afforded you. Either out loud or in your mind, say words of gratitude that this purpose was yours for so long.

Each night, move the glass candle closer to the opposite wall. Each night, say words of thanks and gratitude. Then snuff out the flame and relight it the next day.

On day three, as you move the candle, say words of gratitude for the new opportunity. As you move closer to the east wall, invite all the new experiences into your life.

On the seventh day, let the glass candle burn until it goes out on its own. Focus on the image that represents your new calling. Spend a few minutes meditating on the change and welcome it with an open mind.

89: Next Step Spell

Sometimes choices get made for us. You may find yourself suddenly forced to move on from a job, role, or position that you held for a long time. When this happens, you, like many others, may find yourself asking, "What do I do now?" Choice is always the final determination of where your life goes. This spell can help you make that choice by letting you see clearly the paths in front of you.

What You Will Need

+ 3 ribbons of different colors
+ A marker with a fine tip
+ 3 taper candles (eco-friendly), one to match each string
+ Matches or lighter
+ A charcoal disc
+ Fireproof container or cauldron
+ Myrtle essential oil
+ Sage, dried and ground
+ A pendulum

Preparation

Before beginning, consider the options you have before you. There is likely one that has been tugging at you, although you might not believe it possible. There is usually a sensible second choice and a third. Write one of these choices on each ribbon. Then tie each string or ribbon around the matching candle. You will be burning these candles, so do not leave them unattended, as the strings can melt or catch fire. For maximum potency, perform this spell on the first night of the full moon.

Instructions

Go to your safe space. Light the charcoal disc and place it in the firesafe container. Anoint each of the candles with oil. Lay them out next to each other, with their ribbons facing in different directions.

Sprinkle some sage onto the charcoal disc. Light the first candle and hold the ribbon in your hand. Say, "Guides and guardians of this land, show me the future I hold in my hand."

Gaze into the smoke from the cauldron. Do not worry if you don't "see" anything. Think about this path and try to notice any sensations you get. Are you at peace? Are you sad? Does this path feel steady? Chaotic? Let yourself receive thoughts, feelings, and ideas without judgment.

Sprinkle some more sage onto the charcoal disc and repeat the process with the second candle and ribbon. Again, let yourself receive any impressions. Repeat the steps after adding sage to the charcoal disc for the third candle. Once complete, let yourself take a few deep, intentional breaths.

Now take out your pendulum. Hold it as you normally would and say, "Show me yes." Observe the way it moves to indicate yes.

Now stop it with your free hand and say, "Show me no." Observe the way it moves to indicate no.

With your pendulum placed above the end of the first ribbon, ask your pendulum, "Is this path good for me?" What is its answer? If it says no, take that candle and ribbon and move it off to the side. If it says yes, leave the candle in place. No matter the answer, move on to the next ribbon and candle.

If you end up with two options that are good for you, pull the pendulum away and say, "Show me how you will indicate the path I should take." It will move (or hold) to show you what this looks like. Take the pendulum to each ribbon and candle, one at a time, and state the option you wrote on the ribbon out loud. It will reveal the path you should take.

Keep in mind that you still have a choice. The pendulum can guide you but not force your hand. What path you take is ultimately up to you.

Put out the two "no" candles and dispose of them by burying them in your front yard or recycling them (they can always be used for ambient lighting later). Let the "yes" candle burn out. Take the ribbon from the "yes" candle and put it someplace where you will see it regularly.

90: Personal Aesthetic Spell

Your personal aesthetic can help you find your magical presentation in the mundane world. When I was a neophyte (more years ago than I care to admit), I thought that witches had to wear black. I later discovered the difference in my personality and power when I wore a gown vs. jeans vs. sweatpants. They brought out different sides of my personality. In this spell, you will use clothing to access sides of yourself that may previously have been hidden. It is a good spell to include friends on. It is meant to be good fun.

What You Will Need

+ A sampling of different clothes, jewelry, and scarves
+ Music
+ 25–50 nouns (preferably found in nature), or 5 per person if you are inviting a large group
+ A safe place for each person to change clothing
+ A camera
+ Snacks and drinks

Preparation

Gather together all of the items you (and your friend) have brought. It doesn't matter if they are too big. It's more fun if some are. Try to get some that are outside of your comfort zone. If you wear all pink, add some browns or black or green. If you never wear dresses, add a few to the mix. Whatever you try on does not have to be included in your wardrobe. The point is to see how different items help you access different aspects of yourself and different universal vibrations.

Put the music on.

Instructions

As you can probably guess, you will be trying these items on. Pick one noun off the list randomly. Let's say you get "tree." Pick an item and accessories that coalesce with the energy of a tree. Green is a good starting point, but what else could you do? Long sleeves? A lilac scarf to bloom in the spring? If you get the noun "lion," what could you do differently? Try to add the personality of the person, place, or thing into the mix. A doctor has a different aesthetic than a gemstone. How can actions and tone of voice add to the aesthetic?

To mix it up, put two together randomly—"submarine aardvark," "pomegranate kangaroo," "river cliff"—and see what you come up with. Enjoy the snacks while you try on the clothes.

After each round, take a picture. If you're doing this with others, share which ones felt most similar to you. Which ones felt the most different? Did any of the results surprise you? Keep the pictures so you can remember what each felt like long after the spell is over.

91: Open Mind Spell

A mind with a door that only swings open one way is still a closed mind. For a mind to be truly open, we need to be able to think critically about our viewpoints and the viewpoints of others. Think about that for a moment. I chose to include this spell because, more and more, we are living in a divided world. This "you either agree with me or you are my enemy" mentality (us vs. them) is damaging to humanity. Whoever "us" and "them" are, we should be challenging ourselves to try to understand—though not necessarily agree with—opinions contrary to our own. While I am going to avoid discussing any particular ideologies in this book, I encourage you to look for gray areas in the world. This spell is designed to help you do just that.

What You Will Need

+ 3 tall gray candles (off-white or tan can be substituted)
+ Lighter or matches
+ Rosemary essential oil
+ A sheet of paper
+ A pen or pencil
+ A timer
+ A firesafe container

Preparation

Pick a topic that is a little controversial for you but not a hot button issue. For example, if you are a staunch advocate for animal rights and talking about the topic gets you all worked up and in a heated discussion, start with something else. Pick a topic that you care about, but one that you think you can explore with impartiality. Remember, you are not trying to "solve" the issue with this spell, just explore a viewpoint other than your own.

Set the three candles in front of you in a triangular shape. Dab a little rosemary oil on the tops, just below the wicks.

Instructions

On the sheet of paper, draw two lines down the page so that it is split into three equal-ish sections. Write a short description of the controversy at the top in an impartial way. For example, write "Puppies" not "Why puppies are good/bad." In each column, write one of the following subheads: "My POV," "Those who disagree," and "Common ground." "Common ground" should be the center column. "My POV" will correspond to the side of your dominant hand. "Those who disagree" will correspond to your nondominant hand.

Dab some rosemary oil on the area of your third eye (center of your forehead).

Now light the first candle, the one on the side of your dominant hand, and say, "The side I see."

Visualize the light from this candle entering into the column called "My POV." Let it fill up that column.

Next, light the candle on the side of your nondominant hand, and say, "The side I don't see."

Visualize the light from this candle entering into the column called "Those who disagree." Let it fill up that column.

Finally, light the middle candle and say, "The side we both agree on."

Visualize the light from this candle entering into the column called "Common ground." Let it fill up that column.

The next part can be done in one of two ways: you can either set a timer for ten minutes and write in each column for ten minutes, or you can set it for thirty minutes and write on the whole sheet, trying to list as many as possible in each row.

In the "My POV" column, write all the reasons you agree with the topic. Using the example of puppies, you might write, "They are cute" and "Dogs are loyal." In the "Those who disagree" column, write all of the cons. Still using the puppy example, this might include "I'm allergic" and "They cost money." In the "Common ground" column, you are going to write down all of the areas you think the two sides would agree on. In this case, you might write "They are companions" and "Protective." Try not to overthink this too much. This is not an exercise where you have to get it "right"; it is to train your brain to view complex issues rationally.

When you have reached the end of the writing time, review the list. Read each column out loud. How does saying each item make you feel? Read the columns in any order. When you get through a column, rip it from the page and light it with the corresponding candle flame. Then let it burn in the firesafe container. As the paper burns, reflect on what you have learned from that part of the exercise. Repeat the lighting, burning, and reflecting steps for the other two columns individually.

After this exercise has concluded, spend the next few days considering what topic you want to try next. Perhaps you are ready to go on to a tougher topic? Perhaps not. But the more often you do this spell, the more able you will be to understand different mindsets.

92: Mindful Nutrition Spell

Our bodies want to exist in homeostasis, which is a state of balance. When our bodies get enough water and nutrition, they are less prone to diseases, especially chronic diseases. I don't want to intimidate anybody here. Little changes make a big difference. Eating with intention makes a difference. For this spell, I want you to pick one area of your diet that you could improve on. Pick something challenging but manageable, like drinking more water per day. But make the goal measurable. Instead of "more," make the goal of drinking 11.5–15.5 cups of water per day (2.7–3.7 liters), depending on if you are male or female.[9]

What You Will Need
+ A wet- or dry-erase marker
+ Your favorite essential oil
+ A sheet of paper with a calendar or a tracker app on your phone

---

9. "Water: How Much Should You Drink Every Day?" Mayo Clinic, Mayo Foundation for Medical Education and Research, October 12, 2022, https://www.mayoclinic.org/healthy-lifestyle/nutrition-and-healthy-eating/in-depth/water/art-20044256#:~:text=The%20U.S.%20National%20Academies%20of,fluids%20a%20day%20for%20women.

- 7 chime candles, green or gold
- Lighter or matches
- A seed from a plant native to your area (preferably an edible plant, if available)

Preparation

Write your goal on your mirror with a wet- or dry-erase marker. Write it in the present: not "I will do x, y, and z," but "I replace one junk food snack with a fruit each day." For this ritual, you will call on the Greek goddess of grain, Demeter.

Instructions

Every morning, look at your goal. Dab a little essential oil on your wrists. Say, "Demeter, great goddess of grain. Today is a day for doing what is good for me. My goal is [state goal]. Help me to attempt it. Help me to achieve it. Help me to try again, should I succeed or fail. Let my progress be remembered and known. Blessed be."

Each evening when you are home, record on your calendar if you were successful. If you weren't, did you come close?

Anoint a candle with oil and say, "A gift for Demeter in gratitude for her guidance."

Light the candle and let it burn down.

On the seventh night, plant the seed in a natural, public area in offering.

Repeat this spell at least once a month. If you achieved your goal, set a more difficult one the next time.

93: Candle of Intention

I love lighting candles for any reason or no reason at all. Sometimes, though, it is not possible or convenient to have a burning candle around, like at work, for example. When you are at work and you need a bit of focus or luck or patience, you can utilize an electric candle and a bit of essential oil to perform a quick spell. This one is to help you articulate what you mean to coworkers, but you can adapt it for many purposes.

What You Will Need
+ 1 electric candle (with batteries)
+ Lemongrass essential oil

Preparation
Have your presentation or work documents in front of you. If you have blinds in your office, close them. If not, this can be done in the bathroom or at your desk if you feel comfortable.

Instructions
Set your candle on the papers or in front of your computer. Focus your intention on what you need. See yourself being articulate and clear. Take a breath in, then dab some oil on the wick. Breathe out, and "light" the candle. Let the candle "burn" in a desk drawer or other safe space. It can stay lit until your task is complete.

94: Dreaming a Wise Mind Spell

Our dreams are powerful ways to access our inner mind. Each night when we go to bed, our brains work out issues and problems from the previous days. In this way, our dreams bring us a wisdom we can't always access when we are awake. To have a wise mind means to be able to look at any subject and remove what we want to be true from what is true. Perceptions are important, but they should not override fact and logic. This spell can be done whenever you need some perspective or clarity on a situation. It involves your dreams, so don't expect instant answers. And be prepared to do some decoding. This spell will take place over three nights.

What You Will Need
- A piece of lodolite or amethyst
- Lavender essential oil
- A dream journal and pen or pencil
- 3 lavender chime candles

Preparation
Do all of your nighttime rituals. Then, before bed, draw the water symbol on your stone with the essential oil.

Instructions
Hold the stone in your hand. Call out to Melusine three times. State the issue you want wisdom on. For example, "Should I stay with my career path?" Then say the following chant:

> *Melusine, wise dreaming mind,*
> *Bring me wisdom in my dreams tonight.*

Place the stone under your pillow or in your pillowcase.

When you wake up, write as much down as you remember, particularly that which relates to your question.

Anoint the first chime candle with lavender oil and let it burn throughout the day.

Repeat the steps two more times over the next two days. By the third day, you should have your answer. Burn the last candle as thanks to Melusine.

95: Bad Habits Spell

Each and every one of us has bad habits. Some, such as nail biting, might be annoying, whereas a habit of hopping from relationship to relationship can have further-reaching implications. For the following spell, have your energy equal or greater to the level of habit you are trying to break. For example, if you are trying to break a daily habit, you will need to work at it every day. If you are trying to break a habit that you do multiple times per day, you need to work on it multiple times per day (or more). Since breaking a habit can take a minimum of eighteen days, though often more, this spell is designed to take place over twenty-eight days, from new moon to new moon.[10]

What You Will Need
- 28 slips of paper
- A pen
- A box or jar big enough to hold the pieces of paper
- A charcoal disk
- Lighter or matches
- A cauldron or firesafe container (for day 28)

---

10. Phillippa Lally, Cornelia H. M. van Jaarsveld, Henry W. W. Potts, Jane Wardle, "How Are Habits Formed: Modelling Habit Formation in the Real World," *European Journal of Social Psychology* 40, no. 6 (October 2010): 998–1009, https://doi.org/10.1002/ejsp.674.

Preparation

It may be tempting to try to pick out every perceived bad habit that you have and work on them all. Don't do that. Instead pick one, just one, for now. You can repeat this spell for other habits later.

Start this spell on the night of the new moon.

Instructions

With your bad habit clearly in your mind, sit in your safe space.

Take out the first slip of paper and write your bad habit on it with the pen. Try to pick one or two words to describe it, such as "nail biting" or "compulsive shopping."

Hold the piece of paper in your hand and say, "Twenty-eight days, [your habit], gone away."

Put the paper in your box or jar.

As you go through your day, be mindful of the habit and do something else instead.

The next day, repeat the process of writing on the paper and putting it in the box or jar. But this time, say, "Twenty-seven days, [your habit], gone away." Again, be mindful of the habit you are trying to break, and try to divert it when it arises. This is an important part of the spell and should not be overlooked.

Each day when you repeat this spell, remove one number from the time: twenty-seven days, then twenty-six, and so on.

On the last day, start a charcoal disc in your cauldron or firesafe container. Repeat the steps just like you did on the previous night. Then pull out all of the pieces of paper.

Light them on the disc (you can use matches if they won't light). One by one, burn the paper and say,

> [Your habit] is gone, forever it is away.
> I [your habit] no more.

Let them smolder. The next day, after the ashes have completely cooled, give them to the earth, knowing that your habit is being transformed into something useful and new in Mother Earth's womb.

96: Blessing Jar Ritual

This is a spell that is constantly flowing. The best time to start a gratitude jar is on an annual milestone, such as New Year's Day, Samhain (Halloween), or your birthday. If possible, you want to pick a day with significance so that you remember to renew and redo it every year. Put the jar someplace you can see it and it will serve as a visual reminder of life's bounty.

What You Will Need
+ A good-sized jar with a lid
+ A knife
+ Paint, markers, and other things to decorate the jar with
+ Glue or tape
+ Several pieces of paper (construction paper works well)
+ A pen
+ A notebook or journal

Preparation
First, prepare your jar. It should be clean and dry. Cut a hole in the lid with a sharp knife, scissors, or a can opener. Then put the lid back on.

Next, you can decorate your jar. I recommend putting "gratitude jar" or "blessing jar" on the jar, but this is completely up to you. Once the jar is decorated, set it in a place where you will see it every day.

Instructions
Every time something good or that you are grateful for happens throughout the year, write it on a slip of paper and stick it in the jar. At the end of the year (or whatever date you have chosen), pull out the pieces of paper and read them one by one. Some people like to make a scrapbook or keep an electronic list of these gratitude slips.

Reuse your jar every year and notice how it gets fuller and fuller each time. This helps train your brain to focus on the amazing, good, and inspiring things that happen in your life. Throughout the year, the slips of paper can serve as a visual reminder that things are not as bad as they seem.

97: Winds of Change

The winds blow all over the planet. Since the days of ancient Greece, tales have been told of the winds bringing about change. You can harness this to your magical advantage. According to Greek mythology, the four main winds are named Boreas (north), Notus (south), Eurus (east), and Zephyrus (west).[11] In this spell, you will call on them to bring about change in your life.

What You Will Need
+ A stretch of clothesline or rope
+ Several squares of cloth or flags, at least 1' x 1', though larger is better
  - 1 purple
  - 1 vibrant orange (like autumn leaves)

---

11. "Anemoi/Venti," Collections Online, The British Museum, accessed June 16, 2023, https://www.britishmuseum.org/collection/term/BIOG206272#:~:text=The%20Anemoi%2C%20or%20winds%20gods,%2C%20Favonius%2C%20Auster%20and%20Vulturnus.

- 1 yellow
- 1 pastel blue
+ A Sharpie (Paint can be used, alternatively.)

Preparation
This spell needs to be done outside, preferably on a windy day. You will need two trees or poles to tie your rope to. Try to find a spot that would be undisturbed if you left your flags unattended. It is a good idea to scout the area beforehand and make sure you have enough rope to tie between two trees. It adds extra oomph to your spell if you can face the direction of each wind while you are calling to it, but this is not a requirement.

Instructions
Lay out your length of rope on the ground in front of you. Take your first square, the purple one, and lay it out flat. You are going to write the name "Boreas" on it. While you do this, you will chant,

> *Northern wind,*
> *Winter chill.*
> *Bring changes to me*
> *That allow me to heal.*

Tie this cloth to your rope. Then pick up the orange flag. Write the name "Eurus" on it while you chant,

> *Winds of south,*
> *Winds of east.*
> *Clarity on things I seek.*
> *Eurus, bring this change to me.*

Tie this cloth to your rope. Then pick up the yellow flag. Write the name "Notus." As you do so, chant,

> *Southern winds,*
> *Southern sky.*
> *Winds of Notus,*
> *Bring wisdom to my life.*

Tie this cloth to your rope. Then pick up the blue flag. Write the name "Zephyrus." As you do so, chant,

> *Western winds blowing in,*
> *Intuition is now given.*
> *Zephyrus, winds of youth,*
> *Bring this change about.*

Tie this last flag to your rope. Then tie your rope to the two trees you previously found. Let the flags flap in the winds for twenty-four hours. Then bring the rope inside and hang the flags in their respective corners of your home.

Once per season, tie them back to the rope and let them blow in the winds to recharge their energy of change.

98: Lightning and Thunder Spell

When you need a direct and focused yet intense bit of energy for a project, you will have it at hand using this spell. But don't get struck by lightning; the point is to harness the energy, the electricity, in the air. You will be collecting it, in a sense. This spell can only be done during a storm, but it can be done from relative safety. In other words, when there is a storm, do not go stand under the tallest tree you can find. Instead, just open a window or patio door.

What You Will Need
+ 3 copper coins (cleaned with soap and water and dried)
+ A jar with a lid, filled halfway with water (all the better if it is rainwater from a previous storm)
+ 7 candles for lighting
+ Lighter or matches
+ A hand drum

Preparation
Right before the storm rolls in, put the copper coins in the jar. Set the jar outside, preferably someplace with an unobstructed sky. Put the lid under the jar. Wait for the storm before moving on.

Instructions
Light the candles so that they surround you and your drum. Each time there is thunder, beat your drum. Try to get a feel for when the thunder will sound, and beat your drum in sync with it. Each time lightning strikes, see that energy entering the jar and the copper coins it holds.

When the storm starts to subside, bring the jar back in. Remove the coins and put the lid back on your jar. You can use the coins each time you need the power of lightning and thunder.

99: Thinking beyond the Ordinary Meditation

This meditation will encourage you to think beyond the ordinary. It is related to creativity, but where creativity usually involves the creation of something new, this spell involves seeing ordinary things in a new way. We are surrounded by mundane items, but this does not mean we are limited to using them in mundane ways. This may lead to creative endeavors in the process. You will need three ordinary items: a spoon, a pencil, and a key. Each of the items seems an ordinary item with a mundane purpose but can be repurposed and given a magical task.

Begin Meditation

Pick up the spoon. Hold it flat in your palm and look at it. Bring your attention to how it feels. Is it smooth? Cold? Metal? Wood? When you have spent some time with the spoon, close your eyes and visualize it in your mind's eye. At the tip of the spoon, you see a blue strand of light. You begin to pull the strand of light as if you are pulling a boat to shore. As you pull the strand of light, you see someone using a spoon to eat their breakfast. You keep pulling, and you see someone playing the spoons on their knee.

As the cord of light gets pulled in, you become aware that you are traveling back in time, seeing all the ways that spoons have changed and been used over decades, over centuries. You see spoons on noses and at dinner parties. You see a spoon giving medicine to a sick child. Look at all the ways spoons have been used throughout time. Keep pulling the thread until you come to the moment when the first spoon was created thousands of years ago. What are some of the uses that surprised you? What are some you expected?

Begin to slowly let the line of light back out. When it is taut, set the spoon down and bring your consciousness back to your room and to the next item. Pick up either the pencil or the key and repeat the steps you did for the spoon. Then do the same for the remaining item.

This meditation should help you to see mundane items in a new light and think of ways to use them that never would have crossed your mind previously.

100: Daily Accountability Meditation

It is not pleasant to admit when we are wrong, but growth and the right thing aren't always pleasant. In order to learn from mistakes, we have to make them. That being said, we don't have to dwell on them. This spell uses meditation to help us reevaluate our day. It should be done right before bed.

Begin Meditation

Start by bringing your attention to your breath. Think back to when you woke up. Replay your day to the best of your ability. Were there moments when you were frustrated? Short-tempered? Selfish? Needlessly crass? Make a checklist of each of these times. You may have many. Some days you may have none. When you find one, think back to how it impacted your body, mind, and spirit. Did it feel heavy? Chaotic?

Take a deep breath in, then a forceful breath out. On the out-breath, release all of the tension caused by this experience. One by one, go through each experience and play out, in your mind's eye, what you would like to do next time. How does this seem to impact your body? Your mind? Your spirit?

Be willing to learn from these experiences and not judge yourself for them. They are part of life, and luckily, we can improve and change and adapt and grow to handle stressful situations in a more well-rounded and beneficial way.

Chapter 9
Reconnecting

We are part of an energetic force that connects all things. Throughout this book, you have learned how to connect to yourself through knowledge, archetypes, and exploration. In this chapter, you will learn how (and when) to connect to things outside of yourself. We are a part of nature, not apart from nature. Too often, though, we humans forget this and see ourselves as existing outside of the natural universal rhythms.

When you begin to look beyond the self and see how you fit into the universal macrocosm, you start to understand how some seemingly small act can have wider repercussions. You will begin to see how your actions and thoughts influence and are influenced by the world you inhabit.

101: Plug and Unplug Meditation

We live in a connected world. And while this affords us many opportunities to learn, create digital careers, and connect in ways that were inconceivable fifty years ago, it can also overload us. This meditation will help you to unplug temporarily from the world so that you can connect to the Divine within and all around. You will be plugging into the natural world.

If possible, use candlelight instead of electricity in the room you are going to be meditating in. The less electricity you are using, the more you will unplug and the more effective this meditation will be. If you like to have music while you meditate, choose something instrumental and have the source be outside the room.

Begin Meditation

Get comfortable and close your eyes. See yourself sitting on a plateau, high above the valley below. There is a river flowing, wind blowing. The sun is just peeking over the horizon. It is warm enough to evaporate the dew off the grass that surrounds you but not to remove the crispness of night. The moon still hangs as a sliver in the sky.

As you sit here, become aware of a plug that connects you to all the digital technology in the world. Reach back and gently pull this plug out of your head, knowing that it will not harm you to remove it. As you hold this plug in your hand, become aware of the world around you: Birds singing their morning songs greet you. The smell of daffodils invigorates your mind. The world has become clearer than it has been in months, maybe years.

Look down at the cord you hold in your hand. Once so controlling, it now lies still and empty, without any hum of electricity flowing through it. Since nature does not waste, this plug will be repurposed. First, plunge it into the river below. This cleanse begins to transform the cord, cleansing away all the toxins it once contained.

Now roll this cord into the earth, letting the minerals contained in the wires pick up the resonance of the planet. Hold this cord/root up to the sun and let it be charged with the cosmic energy of fire contained in the life-giving, glowing orb. As you make your way through each of the four elements, it looks less like some man-made thing and more like the root of a mighty tree, the roots of our mighty selves.

The final element is air. As you let the breeze tease its way around the root, you become aware of the great human connection. You become aware that every rock and every drop of water and every bird, fish, and amphibian—that all things—are part of you and part of one another.

Let this root attach itself to you so that it may serve as a reminder to unplug from technology from time to time and plug into the energy of the earth and the stars—energy that is immeasurable in age and power.

When you are ready, begin bringing yourself back to the mundane world. Sit and be present in your tech-free space for as long as you are able. And know that as you go through your day, you have established a connection that is cosmic and primal.

102: Speak to Plants Spell

Humans used to be able to communicate with plants, not with words as we would speak to each other now, but through the language of energy. There isn't much evidence to show how wise men and women of the past learned to use herbs for healing, but I believe the ability to understand them on an intuitive level played an important role. If you don't already have conversations with plants about the nature of the universe, knowing how to speak to them can help you tap into other natural energies in the mundane world.

What You Will Need

+ A living plant, preferably one you take care of
+ A notebook

+ Pen or pencil
+ Plant food or coffee grounds
+ Water or access to water

Preparation

If you have never had a conversation with a plant, it can seem awkward at first. It may help to have a list of questions or conversation topics at hand. I've listed some here as examples, but you are invited to write your own.

+ "What is your name?"
+ "What environment do you like?"
+ "Are you a medicinal plant?"
+ "Are you poisonous?"
+ "How do you protect yourself from predators?"
+ "What is the plant wisdom you have to impart?"

Instructions

Focus on your breathing for several minutes to enter an altered state of consciousness. Bring the plant into your ritual space or join it outside. What you are trying to establish is a friendship with this plant. Start by introducing yourself to the plant as you would a friend. Ask the plant its name, then listen with your intuition for the response. You might find it helpful to touch the dirt around the plant. Sit in the space, ready to receive any information. Write down any impressions of the plant that you get. Does your body feel hot or cold suddenly? Do any colors flash across your mind? What about words or images? Write down any and all impressions.

Move on to the next question and repeat the process. Are there some questions that get a quicker response? Some that don't get any response? Make note of these as well. Make your way through all of the questions, but be open to just having a conversation as well. Try not to force anything.

Record your impressions. Then give the plant food or coffee grounds as an offering to the plant. If it is thirsty, give it the gift of water—a thank-you for sharing its wisdom with you.

103: Speak to Plants Meditation

The steps for this meditation will be similar to the spell. It works best if you use the same plant you have established a rapport with. You will situate yourself near the plant and enter a meditative mindset. Close your eyes. Place your hand at the base of the plant. You are going to listen or look for vibrations or colors around the plant. When you speak words to the plant, they should be something simple that the plant could understand, either something it encounters like "earth" or "water," or a universal concept like "growth."

Begin Meditation

Speak a word to the plant. When you speak, see your voice turn into waves, a visible pattern you can see. Maybe it is smooth, or it could have color. This vibration reaches the plant.

As you speak, gaze through the plant. You don't want to stare at the plant, but let your eyes soften. If you have experience with reading auras, this is the effect you are going for. If not, you are looking for the energy field around the plant. Remember, you might not see it. You might instead experience it with some other senses. When you say "earth," what sensations do you get from the plant?

Change the word. Again, use something a plant can understand, and see your words form as a wave or pattern. What changes for the plant?

Once you practice this a few times, you can begin to have conversations with the plant. Start simple. Ask the plant, "What will you say when you need water?" Listen for the answer. If you don't get the answer, ask again. This takes practice, so don't get discouraged if you don't receive answers the first time. Magic takes work.

Record the answers you receive so that you can track your progress.

104: Heartbeat of the City Meditation

Pagans have a natural connection with wild places and green spaces. But we should always remember that the city has a magic of its own, and I don't just mean in the green spaces. The tube rumbles beneath my feet. The buses pull up and stop and go. The concrete heats and cools. All of these things are the transformation of energy. That is what magic is. Do not despair if you live in a concrete paradise; there is still magic to be found if you know where to look for it. I live in an old city. The people who have lived here before me have left their energetic markers. The people who live here now leave footprints, both physical and ethereal. You can tune in to the heartbeat of the city you live in with this meditation. Start by going to one of the quieter parts of your city. It doesn't have to be desolate, but you should avoid the city's center to start with. Parks are an excellent starting point, but only one option.

Begin Meditation

You are going to engage each of your senses, starting with sound. Close your eyes. Let the sounds around you come to your attention. What do you hear? A vehicle? Birds? Children playing? Do any of them repeat in a pattern? Focus on one, preferably one with a pattern, and try to hear only that sound.

Without opening your eyes, touch the earth beneath you, even if it is concrete or metal or dirt. While still focusing on the sound, let your attention come to the ground. How does it feel when the sound repeats? How does it feel when the sound doesn't repeat? Let yourself connect the feel of the earth to the sound you are focusing on. When you feel you have done so, move on to breath.

With your eyes still closed, with your ears still homed in on the sound, and with your hands still touching the earth, start breathing with intention. Breathe in and out through your nose. What do you smell? Does it match the sound? The feel? Try breathing with the repeated sound. Does anything change? If so, what?

After a few breaths in through your nose, begin breathing through your mouth. Can you taste the air? Does it match the smell? Does it seem symbiotic with what you are feeling, hearing, and smelling? Does it change when the sound repeats?

Now there is just one sense left. Before you open your eyes, check in with all the senses you just used. Locate the sound. Touch the earth. Smell and taste the air. When you have located these senses again, slowly open your eyes. What do you see? How does it connect to what your other senses perceived? All of these senses, when engaged in such a way, should help you to recognize the heartbeat of your city and find the magic housed within it.

105: Spell to Find Your Patron God or Goddess

One of the most commonly asked questions for the novice Pagan, Wiccan, or witch is "How do I know which gods and goddesses to work with?" There will be one (or more) that you feel drawn to. This is a good place to start. If you don't feel drawn to one in particular, consider if you are drawn to an era or period of time: for instance, ancient Greece or Egypt or Scandinavia or Rome. Once you have a general idea, you can ask your patron to reveal themselves to you. Keep in mind that over the course of your lifetime, you may find that your patron changes. This is common and nothing to worry about. The gods call to us as they see fit.

What You Will Need

+ A representation of the pantheon you think your deity belongs to (You might find a pyramid for Egypt, a frog for Mesoamerica, or a triquetra for Celtic traditions.)
+ A list of gods and goddesses from that pantheon (It does not have to be comprehensive, just those you feel drawn to. Have each name on its own piece of paper or notecard.)
+ A pendulum
+ A pencil

Preparation

Lay out the god and goddess names in front of you. Place the cultural representation on either side of the list. You should be able to rest your elbow on the floor or table and have it hang naturally over the pieces of paper so that when your pendulum hangs from your hand, your arm is supported by the table or floor.

Instructions

Take out your pendulum. Hold it in one hand so that it dangles and does not touch the floor or surface of the table. Using your voice of power (see chapter 4), say to your pendulum, "How will you show me my patron, Divine?"

Watch for your pendulum to move. It may move in a circle or sway. Whatever pattern it makes, pay attention. It may be helpful to mark the symbol on a piece of paper, especially if you are new to working with a pendulum. Here's an example of what yours might look like.

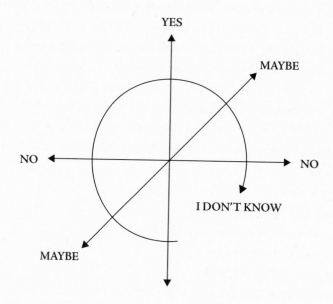

Stop your pendulum with your hand. Now, also in your casting voice, say, "How will you show me those not for me?" Once again, make a note of the pattern.

One at a time, hold your pendulum over each piece of paper or notecard. Say the name of the deity and ask if this is the god or goddess you should work with. For example, "Cernunnos, are you the god calling for me?" Go through each card. You may find a god or a goddess right away, or you may end up with several "yes" answers. If you end up with more than one god or goddess, separate them and repeat the process. But this time, ask, "Are you my patron?" You can still work with the other deities. Your patron is the primary deity you will work with, but you are not obligated to only work with that god or goddess.

106: Ritual to Honor Your Patron God or Goddess

Here is where you get to have a little fun and create your own ritual. You read that correctly. This spell will involve you creating a ritual to honor your patron god or goddess. The first step will be to do your homework. Read the myths that relate to your deity. Can you pick out themes? Patterns? I know the internet makes searching easy, but often the best information about a particular god or goddess will come from going back to the original myths or research done in books. Make a list of common colors, shapes, themes, animals, and anything else that pops out as important while you are researching your deity.

What You Will Need
+ An herb or oil that corresponds to your deity
+ Pen and paper or art supplies
+ A food they might like
+ *Optional*: statue or images to represent your deity of choice

Preparation
Pick a day of the week, preferably one that corresponds to your deity. Then write a poem or piece of prose, compose a song, or paint a picture for their honor. The important bit is the act of creating it, so don't worry about whether it will be "good" or not. Just create it with your deity in mind.

Instructions
On the chosen day of the week, take the food, art, and herb or oil out into nature. Recite your prose or play your song. Make it a celebration for your patron. Let yourself enjoy the food. The more specifics you can

tie in, the better. For example, you may decide a Tuesday in autumn at sunrise is the perfect time to honor Aurora. You may choose to bring images or statues that reflect your god or goddess. There is no way to do this ritual wrong, as long as you do it with the intent of honoring the Divine.

107: Ritual of Thanks to the Gods

As great as spells are, sometimes I get the most benefit from providing thanks to the gods with an offering. The gods are not genies who grant wishes. Regardless of what form they take for you, we can all mostly agree that they are ancient and deserve respect. Sometimes we tend to ask for things or resort to foxhole prayers and forget to be grateful for what we have. This ritual is all about appreciation for the Divine and the gifts that have been bestowed upon us. You can substitute any deity for the ones that I mention. However, if you do not honor a deity, you can substitute any entity, such as a spirit, guardian, ancestor, etc.

What You Will Need

+ An image that represents a god or goddess you work closely with
+ A taper candle in a color associated with that god or goddess
+ Candleholder
+ Matches or lighter
+ Essential oil (If possible, find one that matches the essence of the deity you are honoring, such as water lily for the Greek Hera or wildflowers for the Celtic Lugh.)
+ A candle carver or boline

Preparation
None.

Instructions
Stand before the image of your god or goddess. Breathe with intention and think about all that they have bestowed on you. Try to think beyond tangible acquisitions, though you can certainly include these. For instance, right along with the new job they helped you get, there could be the serenity to not be affected by the chaos around you, the grace to see yourself in a new light, and the courage to not be weighed down by fear.

Focus on one of these and form a single word in your head. Carve this word onto the candle. If you feel called to carve more than one word, do so. After your candle is carved, anoint it with oil while holding the word in your mind.

Place the candle in the candleholder and set it in front of the representation of the deity. Light the candle and say a few words of gratitude to your god or goddess. These words should be heartfelt and genuine. Take your time if you need it, but try to avoid the urge to write the words beforehand. Just let them flow.

After you have spoken your words, sit or stand in front of the flame and spend a few moments in reverence. When it feels right to do so, say thank you once again and exit the room. The candle can burn until it goes out naturally.

108: Dedication to the Path Ritual

Something to understand about this ritual is that it serves as a mental cue. It isn't about you gaining "permission" from someone or something external in order to practice your faith or walk your path. You are giving *yourself* permission to dive headfirst into Pagan and witchy things. Once you give yourself permission, you can connect to your spiritual path and to the gods in new and deeper ways.

You do not have to continue on the path if you later decide that it is not for you. But like so many things in life, you will gain from this path of exploration what you put into it. So, if you find yourself wanting to dedicate yourself to the Pagan path, you can use this ritual.

What You Will Need

- 3–5 candles for lighting
- Matches or lighter
- 2 seven-day glass candles, one white, one black
- A piece of carnelian
- A piece of azurite
- A piece of black tourmaline
- A feather, ethically sourced and legal to own[12]
- A bowl of earth
- A bowl of water
- A star made out of any flexible material
- Cakes on a plate
- Ale or juice in a chalice
- A small bowl or cup
- *Optional*: bath salts and additional candles

Preparation

Take a cleansing bath. Sit in the tub and feel yourself connected to the water. Add bath salts and candlelight for an enhanced effect. If it is not possible to take a bath, a shower will also work. It is important to be intentional with your bathing though. This isn't just washing; this

---

12. "Migratory Bird Treaty Act of 1918, U.S. Fish & Wildlife Service, accessed February 9, 2024, https://www.fws.gov/law/migratory-bird-treaty-act-1918.

is to prepare your body, mind, and spirit to stand before the gods and goddesses. The more time you can devote to pampering before this ritual, the better. You should approach this ritual calmly, grounded, and centered.

Instructions

Start with your ritual bath or shower. As you exit, dry yourself and walk skyclad (or in comfortable clothes) into the room where you will do your ritual. Begin by lighting the candles that will provide illumination during your ritual.

Check in with your body and mind: Are you grounded? If not, take a few moments to ground and center yourself before continuing.

If you want to cast circle before you begin, do so now.

Light the black glass candle. Say,

> *[Great Goddess or Patron Goddess], wise protector, ancient one,*
> *I ask you here to witness and bless my dedication to the path of the Old Ones.*
> *Hail and welcome.*

Light the white glass candle. Say,

> *[Great God, Lord, Horned One, or Patron God], consort, ancient guardian,*
> *I ask you here to witness and bless my dedication to the path of the Old Ones.*
> *Hail and welcome.*

Hold up the piece of carnelian and with your voice of power, say,

This stone is my past.
I honor it, acknowledge it, learn from it, but am not
defined by it.

Place the carnelian between the two glass candles.
Hold up the azurite and say,

This stone is my future.
I welcome it, embrace it, and allow its potential. I do not
fear it.

Place the azurite between the two glass candles.
Hold up the tourmaline and say,

This stone is my present.
I am grounded, living each moment as it comes. I am
present. I am here.

Place the tourmaline between the two glass candles.

My past, my present, my future.
Dedicated for one full turn of the earth around the sun.

Hold the feather in front of your mouth. Watch it dance as you
breathe, then say,

My breath is air.
The words I speak, I dedicate to my path.
May they reflect the Divine.

Approach the bowl of earth and grab a handful, then say,

> *My body is earth.*
> *I dedicate my body to my path.*
> *May the way I treat it reflect the Divine.*

Approach the bowl of water and place your fingertips in the water, then say,

> *My emotions are water.*
> *I dedicate them to my path.*
> *May the way I acknowledge them reflect the Divine.*

Place the star over your heart and say,

> *My heart and actions are fire.*
> *I dedicate them to my path.*
> *May the Divine be reflected in my deeds.*

Now sit in the candlelight and reflect on the words you have spoken. Reflect on how this dedication will impact your life. Spend some time with the god and goddess you called into circle. Have a conversation with them. Is there anything specific they want you to work on? When you feel ready, you may move on to the cakes-and-ale part of the ritual.

Hold the cake plate, then with a fingertip, touch the cake and say,

> *I am the elements. I am the past, the present, and the*
> *   future. Let me eat and be nourished.*
> *Let these cakes be blessed.*

Tear a piece off the cake and set it aside as an offering.

Put your finger on the rim of the chalice and say,

> *I am the elements. I am the past, the present, and the*
> *future. Let me drink and be quenched.*
> *Let this [ale or juice] be blessed.*

Pour some into the small bowl or cup for the offering.

Eat and drink until you feel grounded. When you are ready, open the circle if you cast it initially and reenter the world. It is appropriate to spend the rest of the evening relaxing and feeding your spiritual self.

109: Gratitude for "No" Spell

I was told once that all spells work, they just don't always work as we intended. In essence, we have sent energy toward an outcome. But sometimes it seems that spells fizzle without completion. I like to think that there is a cosmic override, some elder goddess whispering, "No child, that is not for you." In cases like this, one could stomp their feet and hold their breath and get angry. Or one could simply learn to have gratitude for "no."

If you have read my other works, I talk frequently about the power of saying no. But there is also a power in being told no. "No" is a response. When that is the answer you get from the universe, use this spell to come to a place of acceptance.

What You Will Need
+ A piece of paper and a pen
+ A cauldron or firesafe bowl
+ Matches or lighter
+ Red ink and a quill, or a red marker

Preparation
Write the outcome of the spell that did not come to fruition on your paper.

Instructions
Hold the piece of paper in your hand and think about why you wanted this spell to come to fruition. What did it mean to you?

Write "NO" in red ink across the paper. Now burn it and gaze past the flames. Ask what is meant for you instead, thinking about all the ways your life could still lie before you. Use your senses to divine the answers.

When you feel content with the answers you have been given, say with your soul voice, "Thank you for the no. Thank you for leaving my life open to new opportunities. Thank you for the wisdom to accept that which is not meant for me. So mote it be."

110: 111 Meditation

Here we come to the last two exercises in this book. If you remember from the introduction, 111 is about beginnings and endings. But endings are just another set of beginnings—cyclical, rotating, spinning in a never-ending wheel. While you complete this rotation of 111 magic, know that you are not done changing and growing. You are expansive, like the universe itself.

This meditation is to help you connect to the cosmic strands of the universe. You will begin with a singing bowl. Put on loose-fitting clothing, something you can move in, and get comfortable.

Begin Meditation
Start by humming, low and consistent. Pick up the singing bowl; if you can play, play it. If you don't know how to play it, tap the side

lightly. Change the sound of the bowl and your humming until they resonate with the same vibration. If you are unsure if you are there or not, put down the bowl. Your hands should still be vibrating. Hold them to your cheeks and feel the vibration. This will tell you where your hum should be.

Now you will set the bowl down, off to the side (if you haven't already). Close your eyes if you have not already done so. See yourself in your room. You float up and out into the cosmos, beyond the earth, beyond the sky, out where the stars rule. Hum again, but this time feel it travel through your body. See the solid pieces of yourself move and vibrate. Starting at your head, see your hair and skin and muscles and eyes lose solid form and become energetic vibrations.

This happens in your chest and your arms and your fingers. You are no longer solid. All the pieces of yourself are pure energy. Muscle, skin, and bone vibrate in the cosmos. The rest of your body follows suit: Your hips and knees and feet and toes. All of your bones. Fatty tissue. Organs. All of it ceases to be solid and becomes strings of energy, like music notes or thread or particles. All of these are valid.

Let the part that used to be your toes move toward a nearby star. Let your fingers head for a planet. Do not be afraid; all of these bits of energy are connected at a quantum level. You can call them back at any time, and they will instantly reassemble, no matter how far apart they are. Let these bits wander. You are a spirit form. Explore this space. Search out the vibrations of the cosmos. Do the stars sing? Do the supernovas yell? Does the Kuiper Belt have a melody?

Explore these places. Know that you can travel light-years in an instant, in a thought, in a memory. All movements are instantaneous while you are in energetic form. Where do you go? Do you travel to the beginning of the universe? Do you discover what exists the next star over? Do you float and let yourself drift?

You explore for what could be a minute or an eternity. Then you notice the pieces of yourself are starting to reassemble. But they are not reassembling with just your physical form. They are bringing the energy of the planets and quasars and stars they have visited with them. You can see these strings of light all around. As you resume form, you become aware of the connectedness of all things, of yourself to the energy of all things. These strands of energy begin to swirl around you. They form a boundary but also open you to messages from the universe, from the Divine, from the energy that flows through all things. This energy is immeasurable. But it is within you.

This energetic force begins to carry you back down to the earth, through the sky and any buildings, back until your energetic self has completely rejoined your physical self. Take your time to become conscious of the room you are in. Wiggle your toes and your fingers. When you are back, slowly open your eyes. Tap the side of the singing bowl to bring any pieces of yourself still floating in the cosmos back in full. Eat food and drink water to nourish your body. Rest for the next few hours or the remainder of the day in order to honor the trip you have just been on.

111: 111 Spell

I will end now with a spell to connect the beginning and end of all things. It is apropos that it should be the last spell in this book. As all things begin, so too must they end. But there is so much space in between. Take some time to honor the journey you have been on throughout this book. Recognize that even though this is the last spell in this book, your journey is only just beginning. And now, you have some tools to help you on your way.

What You Will Need

- 3 equal lengths of yarn: one gold or orange, one yellow, and one white (Around 13" is a good length.)
- A safety pin
- A pillow or similar item to pin the yarn to and hold it in place (You can also use your jeans, just don't poke your skin.)
- A statue or picture of any triple goddess such as the Roman Diana (the moon, the hunt, and the underworld) or the Greek Hekate (Maiden, Mother, and Crone)
- Rose essential oil

Preparation

Attach the yarn to the safety pin and attach the whole thing to your pillow.

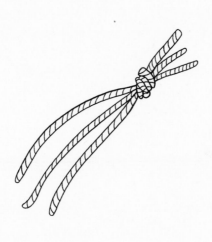

Instructions

In front of you are three golden, glowing strands of light. The white one symbolizes the beginning, where you started. The yellow represents the journey, and the gold or orange one represents the destination, continuously moving.

Begin to weave them together in a simple braid. See the three strands filled with a golden light. While you do so, chant,

> *All things begin. All things end. The journey is more*
> *   important than the destination I seek.*
> *The work I've done, I continue to do; change within me,*
> *   flow all the way through.*

When you get to the end of the threads, knot them together. Then tie the ends together again so that they form a circle. Place this around your triple goddess statue or image. Every week, anoint the statue or image with oil and be reminded that nothing really ends; it just transforms and begins again. When you need an extra reminder, wear the threads around your wrist and return them to the goddess when you are done.

Conclusion

If you have done even a handful of spells in this book, you will hopefully have recognized change within yourself. Change and growth are beautiful things. Though it can be uncomfortable to emerge and become the greatest version of ourselves, the gains far outweigh the costs in the long run. Walking this path will have required some bravery on your part.

If after reading this book and performing some of the magic within, you find yourself stronger, wiser, more able to love, less consumed by anger, or a little more open to life's possibilities, then your work has been a great success.

I encourage you to go out and shape your life into a life of your dreams. You do not need anyone's permission to work on your inner self. You do not need anyone's permission to follow your dreams. Others can guide and instruct, but all of this that you have done to this point has come from within you. And, just as you want those you encounter to respect your boundaries, so too must you respect theirs. For in nature, we must take and we must give. Only by doing so can we understand reciprocity.

No matter what each day brings, we can choose to learn and to adapt. The ability to acknowledge and accept change, even eagerly await it, has been one of the greatest skills I have been able to learn. If you have changed a little or have changed a lot, know that it is just the beginning. Humans are like bodies of water. A pond needs a consistent flow of fresh water to avoid becoming stagnant. So do humans.

May this book have given you the skills to allow change and growth and wellness into your world. May this book be the beginning of a lifelong quest to become empowered through action, through word, and through deed.

Thank you for reading,
Awyn

Glossary

Aesir: In old Scandinavian mythology, the two tribes of gods are the Aesir and the Vanir. The Aesir tend to be more connected to strength and bravery. The Vanir are more closely linked to nature and fertility.

altar: A physical space, such as a bench or desk or table, that is dedicated for magical workings. Not all Pagan faiths and traditions use an altar.

athame: This is a ritual knife that is only used for symbolic cutting on the astral plane. Like a wand, it can be used to direct energy.

chalice: A ritual cup. It is used to hold liquid offerings. It represents the womb and the life-giving properties that come from the womb.

cleansing: To remove all energetic "dirt" from a space.

deosil: A fancy way of saying to move clockwise or sunwise. Opposite of widdershins.

elements: Magically speaking, there are five elements: earth, air, fire, water, and spirit. These are associated directionally with north, east, south, west, and center. Throughout this book, I have chosen to focus on the first four elements to keep the exercises consistent. However, when all four of these elements are together, spirit inevitably follows.

ground and center: This is a practice where you energetically connect to the earth, bring up energy from the earth into your body, and center that energy in your core. It is used because the energy from the earth, in a magical sense, is not finite. If you need to raise energy for spellwork, it is better to tap into an infinite resource than to use your own limited energy.

landvættir: In Norse mythology, the landvættir are land spirits.

Melusine: A female water spirit originating in Europe. Her tale was first written down in the late fourteenth century, though she is believed to have an associated oral tradition long before that. The daughter of a human and a fairy, she was cursed to shapeshift into a half-serpent and later a dragon. Her half-human, half-serpent appearance gives her an association with mermaids.

Norns: Similar to the Greek Fates, the old Norse Norns are Urðr, Verðandi, and Skuld.

Ring-Pass-Not: This is an action or behavior pattern that must be overcome for you to move forward on your life's path. It is usually something that you encounter again and again. It is a barrier to progress.

sitz bones: When you are sitting on your butt with your back straight, your sitz bones are the part of your pelvis that touches the earth. For you anatomy afficionados, they are the ischial tuberosities.

skyclad: To be clad only by the sky. In other words, naked for ritual purposes.

smoke cleansing/smudging: Using smoke from sacred plants to energetically clear a space. Evidence of smoke cleansing has been found in the archaeological record on nearly every continent. Though the word *smudging* is English in origin, it is commonly used to describe similar Native American practices.

Vanir: See Aesir.

wand: Usually, though not always, made of wood. A wand is used to direct energy.

widdershins: A fancy way of saying to move counterclockwise or anti-sunwise. Opposite of deosil.

Recommended Reading

Aswynn, Freya. *Power and Principles of the Runes*. Loughborough, England: Thoth Publications, 2007.

Brockway, Laurie Sue. *The Goddess Pages: A Divine Guide to Finding Love and Happiness*. Woodbury, MN: Llewellyn Publications, 2008.

Calabrese, Joann. *Growing Mindful: Explorations in the Garden to Deepen Your Awareness*. Woodbury, MN: Llewellyn Publications, 2021.

Crow, Granddaughter. *Wisdom of the Natural World: Spiritual and Practical Teachings from Plants, Animals & Mother Earth*. Woodbury, MN: Llewellyn Publications, 2021.

Dawn, Awyn. *Paganism for Prisoners: Connecting to the Magic Within*. Woodbury, MN: Llewellyn Publications, 2021.

Dawn, Awyn. *Paganism on Parole: Connecting to the Magic All Around*. Woodbury, MN: Llewellyn Publications, 2022.

Estés, Clarissa Pinkola. *Women Who Run with the Wolves: Myths and Stories of the Wild Woman Archetype*. New York: Ballantine Books, 1995.

Hutton, Ronald. *Queens of the Wild: Pagan Goddesses in Christian Europe: An Investigation*. New Haven, CT: Yale University Press, 2023.

Murphy-Hiscock, Arin. *The Witch's Book of Self-Care: Magical Ways to Pamper, Soothe, and Care for Your Body and Spirit*. New York: Adams Media, 2018.

Perera, Sylvia Brinton. *Descent to the Goddess: A Way of Initiation for Women*. Toronto: Inner City Books, 1981.

Saille, Harmonia. *The Spiritual Runes: A Guide to the Ancestral Wisdom*. Ropley, UK: O Books, 2009.

Telyndru, Jhenah. *Avalon Within: A Sacred Journey of Myth, Mystery, and Inner Wisdom*. Woodbury, MN: Llewellyn Publications, 2010.

Wolf, Lady. *Skadi: Mother of Wolves and Goddess of Winter*. Somerset, England: Green Magic Publishing, 2022.

References

"All Planet Sounds from Space (Recorded by NASA) | Gingerline Media." YouTube video, 8:37. March 28, 2022. https://www.youtube.com/watch?v=uhGKMh2Bhns.

"Anemoi/Venti." Collections Online. The British Museum. Accessed June 16, 2023. https://www.britishmuseum.org/collection/term/BIOG206272#:~:text=The%20Anemoi%2C%20or%20winds%20gods,%2C%20Favonius%2C%20Auster%20and%20Vulturnus.

Atsma, Aaron J. "Anemoi." Theoi. Accessed February 14, 2024. https://www.theoi.com/Titan/Anemoi.html.

Cherry, Kendra. "What Are the Jungian Archetypes?" Verywell Mind. Dotdash Meredith. Updated March 11, 2023. https://www.verywellmind.com/what-are-jungs-4-major-archetypes-2795439#:~:text=The%20Shadow&text=It%20is%20this%20archetype%20that,prejudice%2C%20hate%2C%20and%20aggression.

Cho, Alethea. "The Ancient Art of Smoke Cleansing & an Interview
    with a Scottish Smudge Maker." Medium and SweetWitch.
    November 28, 2019. https://medium.com/sweetwitch/the
    -ancient-art-of-smoke-cleansing-an-interview-with-a-scottish
    -smudge-maker-6d97f37af899.

"Here's the Best Way to Dilute Your Essential Oils." Abbey
    Essentials. August 4, 2020. https://abbeyessentials.co.uk
    /blogs/news/heres-the-best-way-to-dilute-your-essential
    -oils.

Jeffrey, Scott. "The Ultimate List of Archetypes (Over 325)."
    CEOsage. Updated January 27, 2024. https://scottjeffrey
    .com/archetypes-list/.

Lally, Phillippa, Cornelia H. M. van Jaarsveld, Henry W. W.
    Potts, Jane Wardle. "How Are Habits Formed: Modelling
    Habit Formation in the Real World." *European Journal of Social
    Psychology* 40, no. 6 (October 2010): 998–1009. https://doi
    .org/10.1002/ejsp.674.

"Migratory Bird Treaty Act of 1918." U.S. Fish & Wildlife Service.
    Accessed February 9, 2024. https://www.fws.gov/law
    /migratory-bird-treaty-act-1918.

"Mimir." Encyclopedia Britannica. November 18, 2022. https://
    www.britannica.com/topic/Mimir.

"Saturn." Jet Propulsion Laboratory. NASA. Accessed January 25,
    2024. https://www2.jpl.nasa.gov/solar_system/planets/saturn
    _index.html.

Shakespeare, William. *Hamlet*. Act 1, scene 3. Folger Shakespeare Library. https://www.folger.edu/explore/shakespeares-works /hamlet/read/1/3/.

Viegas, Jennifer. "17th Century Urine-Filled 'Witch Bottle' Found." NBC News. NBC Universal. June 4, 2009. https://www .nbcnews.com/id/wbna31107319.

"Water: How Much Should You Drink Every Day?" Mayo Clinic. Mayo Foundation for Medical Education and Research. October 12, 2022. https://www.mayoclinic.org/healthy-lifestyle/nutrition -and-healthy-eating/in-depth/water/art-20044256#:~:text =The%20U.S.%20National%20Academies%20of,fluids %20a%20day%20for%20women.

Notes

To Write to the Author

If you wish to contact the author or would like more information about this book, please write to the author in care of Llewellyn Worldwide Ltd. and we will forward your request. Both the author and publisher appreciate hearing from you and learning of your enjoyment of this book and how it has helped you. Llewellyn Worldwide Ltd. cannot guarantee that every letter written to the author can be answered, but all will be forwarded. Please write to:

Awyn Dawn
℅ Llewellyn Worldwide
2143 Wooddale Drive
Woodbury, MN 55125-2989

Please enclose a self-addressed stamped envelope for reply,
or $1.00 to cover costs. If outside the U.S.A., enclose
an international postal reply coupon.

Many of Llewellyn's authors have websites with additional information and resources. For more information, please visit our website at http://www.llewellyn.com.